TALES OF THE
NUMINOUS

WORKS BY TY'RON W. C. ROBINSON II

BOOKS

DARK TITAN UNIVERSE SAGA

MAIN SERIES
Dark Titan Knights
The Resistance Protocol
Tales of the Scattered
Tales of the Numinous
Day of Octagon
Crossbreed (Forthcoming)
Heaven's Called (Forthcoming)

SPIN-OFFS
In A Glass of Dawn: The Casebook of Travis Vail
Maveth: Bloodsport (Forthcoming)

COLLECTED EDITIONS
Dark Titan Omnibus: Volume. 1
Dark Titan One-Shot Collection
The Swordman Collection
The Commander Norland Collection
The Chosen Son Collection
The Nano Man Collection

THE HAUNTED CITY SAGA
The Legendary Warslinger: The Haunted City I
Battle of Astolat: A Haunted City Prequel (KOBO Exclusive/Forthcoming)
Redemption of the Lost: The Haunted City II (Forthcoming)

OTHER BOOKS
Lost in Shadows: A Novel
Lost in Shadows: Remastered
Accounts of The Dead Days
The Book of The Elect
Hod
Hallow Sword: Cursed(KOBO Exclusive)
Symbolum Venatores: The Gabriel Kane Collection

ONE-SHOT STORIES
Maveth, The Death-Bringer
Mystery of the Mutant-Thing
Shade and Switchblade
Retribution of Cain
The Mythologists

TALES OF THE
NUMINOUS

TY'RON W. C. ROBINSON II

CONTENTS

CREED: THE CRYPTIC CIRCLE

I

THE BURNING

Deep in the wilderness, afar off from any nearby city or town, The Cult, a group of worshippers cloaked in their black robes and hoods, stand in a circle, surrounding a strange pit that goes deep into the earth. They light incense and toss it into the pit and start chanting. Their chant is of ancient origin and of a language not spoken in modern civilization. From the pit, a fire roared and poured out of the pit, glowing a bright light. The Cult continued their chanting, until something had rushed toward them through the trees. They glanced around while continuing chanting.

From around them came a dark blue shadow, which knocked them from the pit. The shadow moved through the trees, attacking the worshippers. From the trees as the shadow came to a still, a figure arose from the trees. The figure's size was large, its golden eyes glowed in the darkness. Its body was dark as the night, except for a large white cross which covered his entire torso. Burnt bands on its arms and legs. Shining claws on its fingers. The shadow moving through the trees was the dark blue cloak it wore on his back.

"You will not succeed in this ritual." The figure said with a deep, graveling voice.

"Our master is coming." A member declared. "Not even someone of your nature can stop him."

"He can be stopped, and I will be the one to stop him."

The figure moved quickly as lightning and attacked the Cult. Beating them down, leaving them unconscious. Afterwards, the figure walked over toward the pit and looked down, seeing the fire still rising. He placed his dark hand into the flame and it did not burn.

"What is this?"

"Fire from the Cryptic Zone." said a figure behind him. "A place you are familiar with, Creed."

Creed turned around, seeing the angel Ananchel hovering above him. She came down and stepped onto the ground, walking toward him. Her wings were as bright as the sun, yet, a clearing came from them.

"Why are you here?" Creed asked.

"Because this needs your assistance. Adrambadon is near and his powers are growing at an hourly rate."

"And why has no one managed to stop him?"

"Stopping him isn't our task. It is yours."

"You're angels. You should be able to handle the might of the Cryptic Lord."

"Yes, we can. But, it isn't in our master's will."

"So, it's up to me to stop him."

"Yes. And you must do so quickly. As each portal is open, Adrambadon comes closer to stepping foot on the earth once again."

"Is that what this is? A portal into the Cryptic Zone?"

"Yes. They need to be closed."

"How many of them exist?"

"Six."

"How long do I have before he rises up?"

"A few days at most. Soon, his disciples will be upon the earth. Making way for his entrance."

"Disciples." Creed said. "Very well, I will handle them and if Adrambadon does rise from his dwelling place, I will deal with him as well."

Creed evaporated and vanished from Ananchel's sight. She glanced up at the full moon and sighed.

"His anger still kindles within him."

II

<u>THE GATHERING</u>

Creed went and circled the world, searching for every potential trail that could lead to Adrambadon and his rise. During his travel, he could feel within his being, Adrambadon's power growing. He would see the earth shake at every moment, signaling the Cryptic Lord's rise to power and reach toward the earth.

"His power is growing. Faster than even I could anticipate."

Ananchel appeared from behind Creed as he hovered in the air, overlooking the city of London. Where a portal was found in the outskirts of the city.

"He's growing in power." creed said.

"It will be only a matter of time before he surfaces above the ground."

"How do we close these portals?"

"By defeating those who he has placed upon the earth."

"Who's already here?"

"His allies. Forces from realms like his own. There is one that was sighted in Scotland. They call him Abacus."

"A demon?"

"Yes. One who is famous for his earthly appearances through Ouija boards. The generations of Man summon him continually without knowing the damage they're doing to the earth."

"Humans will never learn."

"Something we can agree on."

"I will find him out in Scotland. Summon him myself by using other means than a wooden board."

"And what will you do once he's in your sights?"

"Eliminate him from creation. It'll send a direct message to Adrambadon and his other allies."

Ananchel nodded. "I see."

Creed flew off and Ananchel hovered into the sky, vanishing through a quick sight of light. Creed traveled through the air at the speed of aircrafts, heading to Scotland. While flying, he concentrated his energy to discern nearby dark elements. Sensing nothing, he continued to make his move to Scotland to find the demon Abacus.

In Scotland, Creed flew in the night sky, as he flew, he caught a glimpse of a flashing light ahead of him. Keening his gaze upon it, Creed went toward it. Seeing it's the Callanish Stones. Upon landing on the ground, he discovered the flashing light was in fact a diversion. Only a strange crystal left unguarded.

"I know you're here." Creed uttered.

Behind him appeared a figure. Lean, toned, and dark as coal. Its eyes were white as the stars and it wore a cloak with a ripped tunic. Creed stood before the figure.

"I take it you're the one they call Abacus?"

"I am. I knew you would come. You're much bigger than he had told us."

"Where's Adrambadon?"

"He's on his way here. This world will be his. As will all others."

"A repetitive plan. It's been done before and it failed."

"Not with my maser, Adrambadon. He is aware of the goings of this world. The rising heroes, the change in the scenery, the loss of faith and the drive for individualism."

"The world will change once the end has come."

"Adrambadon is coming to bring the end. Just, not the way you are expecting."

From Creed's arms appeared an axe. The axe was made from his armored suit. Abacus was astounded by the quickness of the weapon's appearance. He gleaned closer to the axe and gasped.

"I recognize that material."

"You should."

"Oh, my. I didn't even notice."

"It's too late now."

"No, it's perfectly shown."

Creed lunged toward Abacus with the axe, Abacus moved from the attack and swerved himself around Creed, attacking him from all points. Creed's cloak swirled up the air around them, knocking Abacus into a set of the stones. His eyes brightened gold and Abacus smiled.

"Good. Good."

Creed grabbed Abacus by his throat and slammed him into

the ground, denting the dirt. Abacus laid in a hole and rose up with a bigger smile on his face. Creed stepped back and grabbed the axe from the ground and slammed it on Abacus' left arm.

"Nice one." Abacus said, looking at the axe in his arm.

"Your head is next."

"I think not. This is only the start and I am needed elsewhere."

Creed swiped the axe across Abacus' neck. Slashing his head from his body. Abacus' body fell motionless and the head rolled over to the stones. Bouncing off of the standing mineral. Blood flowed from the body. Creed placed the axe over his shoulder and as he turned away, the stones glowed a neon blue. The ground started to quake.

"What is happening now?" Creed wondered.

From the stones, the ground had opened to reveal another portal. From the opening a bright light shot up into the air and traveled across the corners of the sky. Creed already knew it had just made a connection to the other portals and he could feel within himself Adrambador was inching closer than before.

III

<u>THE CIRCLE</u>

Adrambadon's presence began to grow upon the earth. Creed could feel it at every second passing. Ananchel appeared before him with a sense of fear moving through her eyes, scattered from across the earth.

"Something's wrong." She said.

"He's coming. Creed replied. "But, I cannot have him reach the surface."

"What are you planning to do?"

"I will enter the Cryptic Zone and face him there. Defeat him at his own turf."

"You cannot. You alone won't be able to defeat him. Especially when he derives his power from the realm he resides."

"What other option do you have?"

"Perhaps we can wait on assistance and face him when he arrives."

"Foolish talk. If we were to take that chance, he would destroy much of the earth and kill those who he wishes. For an angel, you are surely a fool."

"I am what I am."

"You fear Adrambadon and yet, I don't recall you facing him in times past. Or did you?"

"I've seen what he can do firsthand."

"Then, join me in entering his domain and taking him out."

"It can't be just the two of us."

"Call one of your friends from the heavens. See which of them will assist us in this war."

"They're all busy at the moment. There are other things taking place right now."

"Then, while you wait, I will enter the Cryptic Zone."

Immediately in front of them, another angel came down from the sky. His height was tall, and he stood upright with a stature with his arms and feet the color of brass. His eyes kindling with fire. Creed looked up toward the angel. He nodded slightly.

"Uriel." Ananchel said.

"Ananchel, I received the call."

"That fast?" Creed asked.

"Yes."

"I would've expected you to come down here. Where are the others?"

"Michael and Gabriel are busy with matters throughout the cosmos. I came because of the need this quest requires. You plan on entering the Cryptic Zone to face Adrambadon. You will need some celestial assistance."

"This is good." Ananchel said.

"How many friends does Adrambadon have down there?"

Creed asked.

"Other than Abacus, the one they named Satanic."

"It tells enough." Creed said.

"Not exactly. Unlike Abacus, Satanic is more animal than your standard demonic foe. Runs on all fours, equipped with bullhorns and a raging taste for blood. No matter where it's from."

"Good to know. The two of you can handle Abacus and Satanic. Leave Adrambadon to me."

"Are you positive of your choice?"

"I am."

"How do we exactly enter the Cryptic Zone?" Ananchel wondered.

"We jump into one of the opened portals, a direct lead to Adrambadon himself. Or one of you can just open a doorway to his domain yourselves. If you possess the power to do so."

"If we were to do so, Adrambadon will discover us before we enter. Better we use his portals to our advantage."

"Good." Creed said. "Let's go."

They reached a nearby portal and lunged themselves in. diving down into a bright pit. It resembled a bottomless pit as they fell, nothing was dark and heat, instead everything was a bright violet with a cool breeze of air. Continuing their fall, Creed pushed himself further down as the angels followed.

"We're nearing the drop-off." Creed said.

"How do you know?" Ananchel asked.

"See that circle glowing ahead, it is the entrance to the Cryptic Zone."

From there, Creed and the angles landed. The portal above

them still operating and they looked at their surroundings. Covered with orange crystal-like objects growing from the rocky walls. Emitting a strange energy. Creed felt the realm's own energy sinking into his body.

"Looks different than I can tell." Ananchel said.

"Keep your guard up." Uriel said. "They're not as far from us as you would believe."

"You know us well." Came a voice from around them.

They turned around, seeing no one, turning once more and yet there was still no one around.

"This way." The voice uttered.

They turned to its direction and there, they found themselves staring at Adrambadon himself. Besides him were Abacus and Satanic. Creed stared down Adrambadon. Abacus grinned at them and Satanic began to bark toward the angels. Adrambadon sat on a throne made from the same mineral that was seen growing in the walls. He was dressed similar to an overlord. Leathery armor from his neck to his feet. His long hair was in fact streams of fire. His eyes had no pupils. His face could be made out from its own shining streak. His voice echoed deep through the Cryptic Zone.

"Two angels in my realm!" Adrambadon said. "This is a good day."

"You know why we're here." Uriel said.

"Of course!"

"I've come to end you." Creed declared with anger. "Of all the things you've done."

"You can't blame me for the travesties that have grown upon the earth. For I know your true purpose and where your powers lie. Remember."

"I'm not here to discuss history. I have come to end you."

"Give it a go! Many have tried before your time and many will try after you've turned to dust."

Abacus warped and attacked Ananchel as Satanic rushed over against Uriel. Uriel grabbed the beast by the horns and slammed it against the wall, its scaly, burnt hide rubbed against the rocks. Creed stepped forward, facing the Cryptic Lord. Adrambadon stood up from his throne and stepped down its stairs.

"You will not succeed this day." Adrambadon declared.

"I will do what my purpose commands me!"

Creed raised his axe and lunged toward Adrambadon. He held his hand up, freezing Creed in mid-air.

"Then, you should be doing my will. After all, I'm the one who endowed you with the powers you possess. Have you not forgotten? I was the one who gave you this new life, gave you a portion of my own power. You were sent to the earth to do my bidding. The opening of the portals was your task."

"I am not your pawn!" Creed yelled, trying to fight against the hold.

"Oh, but, you are! Instead, you've chosen to help the innocent. Believing it will grant you repentance from your past sins and give you eternal life. What did you expect? You believe the Most High will save you?"

"He has all power in His hand!"

"I am aware. For this universe has so many secrets, not even I know them all. But, I will do what I must until the appointed time arises. For now, I will end you and find a new Creed to put in your place. One that will not disobey my commands."

Uriel flew over and swiped his sword against Adrambadon's chest. Creed fell from the hold and landed on the ground. Ananchel rushed over to him as he stood up.

"Where's Abacus and Satanic?" Creed asked.

"We dealt with them. But, they will be back soon."

Adrambadon grabbed Uriel's sword and kicked him toward Creed and Ananchel. Tossing his sword back to him, Adrambadon approached the three and gazed up toward the portal above them.

"How soothing it will be to have the three of you here with me for eternity. As this portal shall now be shut."

The portal began to close. Creed ran toward the Cryptic Lord, reaching from his back, impaling him with a spear made from his own power. Uriel and Ananchel flew up to the portal.

"Creed, come on!" Ananchel yelled.

Creed turned to Adrambadon and looked him in the eyes.

"Our war isn't over."

"Of course not!" Adrambadon said. "For we will have many battles and then, the war."

Creed pushed Adrambadon back and went into the portal. Adrambadon gazed up and smiled. Starting to laugh as he pulled the spear from his body and healed the wound with one of the orange crystals.

"Another day, my creation."

IV

<u>THE FUTURE</u>

Creed, Ananchel, and Uriel bolted from the portal and as they touched the ground, the portal shut. Its light vanished and the surrounding area silent. Creed looked around, feeling strange.

"This isn't where we last stood."

"The portal must've brought us somewhere else."

"We near a city. One the humans call Washington D.C."

"Why are we here?" Creed asked.

"I don't know." Ananchel said. "But, right now we need to be prepared for Adrambadon's next phase of attack."

"I had him."

"You did not." Uriel said. "Another day, you will."

Uriel and Ananchel hovered in the air above Creed.

"We must return to our domain." Uriel uttered to Ananchel. "We've been away long enough."

"Understood." She said. "Creed, I will return as soon as I can."

The two angels flew off into the sky. Creed sighed and turned around, only to find himself facing an elderly woman who was twice his height. She wore a dark blue dress with white linings throughout it. Appearing to be small crosses. Her hair was white as snow and her features were of a young woman, yet, old.

"Who are you?" Creed asked.

"I am known through the realms as Madam Age and today, I have come to warn you."

"Warn me of what?"

"The future. The near future."

"What of it?"

"A threat is brewing upon this earth. Adrambadon is not part of this. Neither are those you have encounter before. This threat is growing from a mortal man and it is near for his power to rise."

"I don't understand."

"Prepare yourself. Prepare."

I

IN YOUR DREAMS

The Death Chaser, known in the spiritual realm as the Soul of Retribution entered the Dream Dimension to complete a task in defeating a demonic entity referred to as Nightmare. The Chaser entered the dimension on a device, appeared to humans as a hybrid between a motorcycle and a Cadillac. The Dream Dimension was surrounded by a dark-green hue as Nightmare arose from the strange clouds. A large demonic figure with long, dark wavy hair, a goatee, and malevolent glowing green eyes. The Chaser approached the entity without fear.

"Nightmare. Your tormenting is over."

"There is no one who can remove me from my domain." Nightmare declared as his deep voice went through the Dream Dimension like a wave.

"This isn't your domain, demon. This is the realm of the dreamers and you are no permitted entry into this place. It is time to go."

Nightmare roared at the Chaser and lunged out from the

clouds to attack him. The Chaser raised up a steel whip made of Sinfire and swiped Nightmare's hands, pushing him back into the hue. Nightmare's size was of a large stature to the Chaser's own height and size. The Chaser was as a civilian to Nightmare who was near the height of a 10-stoty building.

The Chaser created a whirlwind of Sinfire that grabbed Nightmare from the hue and sucked him in at a quickening pace. The Chaser picked up the whirlwind and tossed it out into a portal, exiting the dimension.

"Nightmare has been removed. For now."

The Chaser left the Dream Dimension and returned to the physical realm. When he made his return to the land of the living, the Chaser reverted to his mortal form as Danny Logan. He took a breath and went on about his business.

II

A KNIGHT AND A WIDOW

Danny went on, walking down an empty and dirty alleyway. While, walking, he caught the scent of perfume. Yet, it was a strange scent. One of the dead with a slight hint of roses. Danny sighed.

"I just wanted sometime alone." Danny uttered.

Shaking his head, his hands twitching and within mere seconds, he transformed into the Death Chaser. A head cloaked in a hood, but his face a skull. Dressed in all black with spikes running down from his shoulders to his wrists. He looked around with a deep fire in his eyes.

"Show yourself!" He yelled.

From the nearby trash can arose a woman cloaked in all black. Her pale skin reflected with the light coming from the moon. A black veil over her face. She approached the Chaser with fear. He gazed upon her face, reaching to remove the veil. As he proceeded, the scent went from her to him. He stopped his hand in mid-air, inching from her veil.

"The scent is you!" The Chaser said. "Who are you?!"

"Just a widow." She replied, pulling out two medium daggers

from her back. "And I'm not alone."

She gazed up to the rooftop of the building and from there came down a man. Wearing an all red uniform. Resembling a military outfit with shades of black with the exceptions of wings in the form of a trench coat. His face hidden by the shadow of his beaked hood. The two stood before the Chaser with weapons in hand.

"We have been searching for you. For your kind." The man said.

"You desire a challenge from me?!"

"It is why we're here." The woman said.

"Then you're as foolish as your ancestors!"

The Chaser whipped out his sin fire, swiping the walls around them. The two stood back, thinking of a plan. The Chaser was consumed with sin fire, flowing all around him and yet, not touching him.

"What shall we do?" The woman asked the man.

"We take him down. By any means."

"Don't be foolish. Surrender now and spare your lives for another day."

"We can't do that. We've been hunting down an soldier of Demonti for some time and we've finally found one."

"Demonti…?" The Chaser said with a pause. "What do you know of Demonticronto?!"

"You're his pawn! Just like all the others we've read about in the books!" The man yelled.

"Books. Have you ever seen Demonticronto? Have you ever faced him? No. Because if you did, you wouldn't be standing here.

Now, tell me what you know about him."

"Strike him now."

The woman rushed toward the Chaser with her daggers. Attempting to stab him and as the daggers came closer, the Chaser grabbed them with one hand, ripping them from her hands. He threw them on the ground and snatched the woman by the throat. Staring into her eyes.

"Don't you hurt her!"

"Keep quiet!"

"Or what?!"

The Chaser released sin fire that snatched the man and slammed him against the brick wall. Holding him in place. He struggled to get free and as he did, the fire quenched tighter. The Chaser turned back to the woman, removing the veil from her face.

"Why have you chosen such a futile task?"

"We're only doing what's right for all creation."

"And what may that be?"

"Stopping you from unleashing Demonti's power upon the earth."

"You do not know who I am, do you?"

"You're the one they call the Hunter. The one who gathers souls for Demonti's use."

"Then you do not know me." The Chaser said, pushing the woman next to the man. "Allow me to tell the two of you who I am. I am the one sent by the Master to cause sinners to repent by the fear of the damned. I am the entity that is sent out to find lost souls and bring them to a dwelling place. I am the one spoken about throughout the ages as the Shadow, the Angel of Death, the Feared Fire. All of creation knows my name as the Death Chaser, the Soul of Retribution!"

"The Death Chaser?" The man questioned. "How?"

"Because your books were wrong, boy. As is your plan to stop Demonticronto. There is only one way to stop him and I am that way."

"Then, let us free from this fire and help us." The woman said. "Help us stop him."

"I can look at the two of you now and perfectly say, you aren't capable of entering such a realm of existence. You would do better to live like the humans. Live out your days in peace. Read the Psalms and the Proverbs. Place them in your hearts. Live and die. As your ashes return to the earth where it was taken."

The Chaser turned away and the woman screamed. He turned back and started at her with anger kindling in his eyes.

"Don't try something idiotic."

"Help us. Please. If not that, teach us. Guide us to understand the spiritual realm."

The Chaser walked over to them on the wall, swiping his hand across the fire to release them from its heated bonds. They were relieved when the fire was gone, and the heat stopped.

"Just help us out." The man said. "We only want to do some good in this world."

"What are your names?" The Chaser asked.

"John Clarkson." The man said." But, my codename is Robin Knight."

"And you, woman?" The Chaser asked.

"My name was lost when I was young. I have been called Widow ever since."

"Were you married in times past?"

"Yes. But, my husband at the time had died."

"How did he fall?"

"A demonic attack. We were only novices when we discovered the spiritual arts. We read much of Aleister Crowley's writings. Tried to imitate his works. We conjured a demon and my husband was killed in the process."

"Did you learn your lesson?"

"I have now."

The Chaser nodded. "Good. Next time do not bother repeating the works of a mage."

"I understand."

"What now?" John asked. "Will you help us stop Demonti?"

"First thing, how do you know Demonticronto is coming to Earth?"

"We came across a strange spirit. It mimicked the sins of the world. Used them to fuel its own power. The spirit told us the world's sins are increasing and Demonti will rise again. This time with all the world ion his side and it would mean the end of all things."

"We're already in the end." The Chaser declared. "Many just have not looked to notice."

"We have to show him where we came into contact with the spirit." Widow told John.

"I agree. We have to bring you to the site of the sighting."

"Very well." The Chaser said. "Go there now. I will meet you there."

"How?" John asked.

"I am not of this world remember."

"Oh. Yeah. I understand."

The Chaser vanished from their sight through a fiery whirlwind. John and Widow went about their way, going to the site of the strange spirit.

III

SIN IS TRANSGRESSION OF THE LAW

John and Widow's travels have brought them to an abandoned building just outside of the local town. There, they came to the entrance and behind them, the sound of a whirlwind came. They turned around, seeing the Chaser walk out of the whirlwind before it vanished.

"This is the place?" The Chaser asked.

"Yes." John replied. "However, we saw the spirit inside."

The Chaser examined the building. He could smell blood, vomit, feces, and gunpowder from its surroundings. He shook his head and rubbed his face.

"This was a slaughterhouse many years ago. Once a gun manufacturer, a prison for children, and a mental institution."

"How do you know all of this?" Widow asked the Chaser.

"The scent is still here. No matter how things are moved from place to place. Its spiritual touch remains. This place is a hell made on this earth and one that shut down for good purpose."

"Then, why was the spirit roaming around in here like it was its own?"

"Because of the activities that occurred within this building Many deaths. Many lies. Many false hopes. Many sins committed Lawlessness ruled in this place."

"You can get all of that just by the scent of the building?"

"The grounds are polluted with sins. Man have come here and transgressed the Master's Law. Fortunately, they are all dead and have been grated passage from my wrath. But, that's the least of their worries from this earth."

"What did you mean by transgressing the Master's Law? Who's the Master?"

"Who do you think?" The Chaser said.

"I'm not certain. There are many masters. Many gods. Many rulers."

"Yes, there are. But, only one manages to outwit them all at their own game"

"How?"

"Because He created all things. This universe. This world. You. Her. Myself. Created all things for his good pleasure and his good pleasure alone."

"You're talking about God."

"Which one is God to you? Better starts using names for identification. Don't want to make an error in the future."

"And that is why we need you to teach us the ways of the spiritual realm." Widow said. "To give us a proper understanding."

'Then, you would have to find yourselves a pastor."

"That's difficult to do these days. Most of them are all prosperity speakers. motivation lists for a vain goal. A cost to live in this world without knowledge of the world to come."

"You know enough as is, woman." The Chaser chuckled.

The Chaser approached the wooded doors and kicked them open. Inside of the buildings was nothing. An empty facility. The three entered and the only thing seen was dirt, hay, scurrying rats, and dried remains of the blood, vomit, and tiny specks of gunpowder.

"This place reeks." John said.

"You couldn't smell it from outside." The Chaser said. "Shows just how much discernment you must learn."

The Chaser continued to look at the building and felt a tug in his spirit. He turned his head quickly, startling John and Widow.

"Something wrong?" John asked.

"Someone else is here."

"Here as in the building or outside? I didn't hear any vehicles."

"Someone not of this earth."

The dirt rattled from beneath John and Widow. The Chaser pulled them from the spot and the ground opened, revealing a strange spirit rising. John and Widow stared.

"That's the spirit we saw." John said.

The Chaser stepped forward as the hole in the ground sealed shut. The strange spirit had the eerie appearance of a man, covered in tattoos. Glowing yellow eyes and unkempt hair. The tattoos however were of wicked acts. Sins of the world. Lewdness, uncleanness, filth, and hatred for the spiritual. The Chaser pointed at the spirit.

"Speak your name!"

"Ah, how I've always wanted to meet a Death Chaser." The spirit said. "This is my day."

"You smell of swine's flesh!" The Chaser yelled. "What is your name, Spirit!"

"I don't have a name. I do have a title."

"Don't test me." The Chaser said.

"I am known as the Sin Phantom. I have been on this earth ever since the Flood. The washed sins of those of the past I have consumed and made my own."

"This spirit's been around since the days of Noah?" Widow asked.

"Appears to be so." John replied.

"What are your doings with Demonticronto?"

"You know? Good. Because, he desires to meet you, Chaser. As does he desire to meet every man, woman, beasts, and child upon this world. He wants to give you all what you truly seek."

"And that is?"

"Freedom. Freedom from the laws that bind you. You desire many things. To do as you wish. Demonticronto has that gift for everyone and is willing to grant it. Only by one request."

"What request?"

"You submit to his will and obey his every word. Look up to him as you would to the Most High."

The Chaser emitted sin fire from his right hand. It glowed with a passion. The Sin Phantom steppe back as did John and Widow.

"I do not like your kind, Phantom. That is why I was created. To destroy pests like you!"

"You may try."

The Chaser threw the fire toward the Phantom and it vanished from the building quickly before the fire to touch him. The chaser moved and ran outside, looking for the spirit. But, it was nowhere to be seen. John and Widow followed him.

"Where could it have gone?" John asked.

"It's close." The Chaser replied. "It hasn't gone far enough."

Somewhere in the mountains, the ground shook and opened. From the opening fire arose and within the flames were souls. Souls made of molten rock. A dozen of them came out of the hole as it shut. There, they stood until the Sin Phantom approached them.

"You sent them."

"As are my words, Phantom." A deep voice said from one of the souls. "These tormented souls are here to do my bidding under your command. Release them against the Chaser and his allies. Stall them until my coming is complete."

"Yes, master."

The voice echoed away. The Sin Phantom directed the souls toward the local town.

"Find the Chaser and his allies. Kill them by any means necessary. For Demonticronto!"

The Tormented Souls made their move toward the town with Sin Phantom overlooking them with a large smile on his face.

IV

<u>AN OLD ENEMY</u>

The Tormented Souls entered the town, frightening the locals. However, they did not harm them by any means as their objective is to find the Chaser, John, and Widow. The Chaser continued his search and came across the Souls. Widow also saw them and was immediately unconformable.

"What are they?" She asked.

"Souls." The Chaser said. "Tormented ones."

'Tormented?" John asked. "By what?"

"By he cares of this world and the cares of this life at one point. Now, they're only tormented by the things they should've done when they were on this side of glory."

John watched as they did no harm to the locals of the town. He felt a slight relief come over him. He chuckled.

"They're not harming anyone."

"They're not here for them." The Chaser said. "They're here for us and us they will meet."

"Do we have to fight them?" Widow asked.

The Chaser turned toward her, handing her the two daggers.

She grabbed them and looked at the Chaser.

"You had them the whole time."

"You need them for this moment. The only way we get out of here is to face the Souls. The Sin Phantom is among them. Leave him to me. The two of you take down as many Souls as possible. I will aid you. You do not need worry."

"Alright then." John said. "I guess this is what it's like entering the spiritual realm."

"You have no clue yet, boy."

One of the Souls turned its head, seeing the Chaser. It screeched loudly to the point of shattering the windows of the nearby buildings and cars. Signaling to the other Souls of their discovery. They ran like animals toward them.

"I'm not ready for this!" John said.

"Gird up your loins like a man and face them!" the Chaser yelled.

"I am prepared." Widow said.

"Spoken like a true warrior."

The Souls eased with speed, and the Chaser warped them with sinfire from his mouth. John extended his coat, transforming it into a pair of red wings. Widow twirled her dagger and they fought off the Souls as they came. The Chaser ran through the horde, grabbing the souls by their faces and slamming them into the ground. One of the Souls bit the Chaser on his shoulder. He only laughed as his shoulder turned to sinfire itself, burning the mouth from the soul.

"Now you know pain!"

The Chaser brought out the sinfire whip and swiped the Souls around him. As if they were lost cattle. The Chaser laughed as he done it. Taking pleasure in destroying the Souls of the damned. On the other side of the fight, Widow was impressive in taking out Souls with her daggers. John flew over them, diving down like an eagle to its prey and back up again. The Chaser scouted the area.

"Phantom! Reveal yourself unto me!"

From there, the Phantom arose from the ground. Staring down the Chaser.

"You called me."

"I want you to send Demonticronto a message."

"I am listening."

The Chaser rushed over like lightning, grabbing the Phantom by his jaw. He held him up as John and Widow took down the remaining Souls with a team effort. They fell to the ground in a pile of rocks. The Phantom struggled to get loose from the Chaser's grip.

"Tell Demonticronto, the end is here, and it begins with him."

The Phantom muffled under his breath. The Chaser laughed.

"And show him my mark, which I give unto you."

The Chaser emitted sinfire from his hand, burning the Phantom's mouth and jaw. Dropping him on the ground, the Chaser raised up the whip and the Phantom scurried away. John and Widow ran toward him, looking around. The Phantom was gone.

"You had him." John said.

"I did. For a intentional purpose."

"But, we need to know where Demonticronto is lurking."

Widow said.

"It's taken care of."

"How?"

"My mark is all that was required. I will know where Demonticronto will be at every moment and he shall know as well."

A week later, John and Widow continued to meet with the Chaser to learn the spiritual realm. While on his own, the Chaser would revert to Danny Logan. There, his travels brought him to Washington D.C., where he learned of a strange occurrence of demonic activity taking place.

"The cleansing shall begin." Danny said, morphing into the Death Chaser once more.

TRAVIS VAIL, SPIRIT-SEEKER: FIRST SINS

I

<u>WHAT CAME BEFORE</u>

Reading through his past investigations and encounters with the otherworldly, Travis Vail, known in the occult circles as the Spirit-Seeker, is researching more of his past encounter with Kamagrauto, the demon who opened his mind to the larger world. After the visitation from Kamagrauto at the Black Raven Hotel and in finding the Mutant-Thing, Vail is curious about the world he's about to enter. A world where the supernatural comes into conflict with the rising heroes. A mixture that will only end in chaos.

Still studying, Vail's phone rang, and he answered with slight haste and ease of movement. His instincts were still kicking. His mind on Kamagrauto's words and his encounter with Abraham and The Swordman.

"Vail speaking."

"Trav, good to hear your voice."

"Ah. Dr. Galen Donovan." Vail said with a smirk. "Same here. Why have you called?"

"I have a case for you. If you're interested."

"What kind of case if I may ask humbly?"

"From what I've learned, it concerns the first sins?"

"First sins? As in the first sins committed after the Fall?"

"Correct."

Vail nodded. "I'm on board. Send me the details and I'll follow suit."

"Will do." Donovan said. "You'll have the information shortly."

Vail hung up and within several minutes, the information was sent to Vail through his email. Reading the files, Vail learned the first sins were moving through the world in slow form. Unusual to his previous encounters in past cases, there was a map attached to the files which detailed the past locations of the sins' movements. Vail packed his gear, what was needed, grabbed his black trench coat and left his lair.

Following the map's layout, Vail went across most of the United Kingdom into France and into Germany. Vail has spoken with several witnesses to the sightings and they explained the sins appeared as one. Embodied to moving around single filed. Whatever it was, it had no motives other than to terrorize and to instill fear into the humans it came across. After each movement it made, the more aggressive it became. From startling humans to torturing them if came close.

"This is something else." Vail noted. "Something far more powerful is at work here than just some series of haunting."

Vail continued his investigations and interviews for the next several days. During those days, Vail began to come across what looked to be plague doctors. Crouched in the shadows to walking past him in crowds. Vail took nothing from it until he managed to see one staring at him from the distance. The plague doctor dressed in an all-black robe. Covered from head to toe with its doctor's mask sticking out of its hood. Vail smirked.

"You think that frightens me, lad? Tell you what, take off that beak and we'll settle this like men."

The plague doctor stood still. Vail waited, yet, nothing came from the doctor.

"Figures." Vail said. "I'm going on about my business. Don't try to follow or you'll end up somewhere you won't like."

Vail contacted Donovan concerning the case and the uprising of plague doctors. Donovan stated the doctors are probably the result of the sins' travels. The doctors are following the path of the sins.

"They may be, but, there's something more to all of this. Something sinister at work."

"Why don't we meet up and discuss our ideas on this case?"

"Sure. Where are you right now?"

"In Italy."

"Let me guess, Venice."

"I'm having a word with Ms. Belinda Grazio. You remember her I presume?"

"I can't forget a face like hers. Anyhow, I'm leaving Germany. I'll be there as fast as possible."

"Take your time. Belinda is patient of your coming."

"She would be."

II

<u>WHAT CAME AFTER</u>

Vail entered the city of Venice near nightfall. Vail had walked through Venice reaching the hotel. When Vail came closer, he could see Donovan standing outside of a door.

"There he is." Vail said walking.

Vail made his way toward Donovan and the two hugged.

"You came quicker than I expected."

"I was on the move right after our conversation."

"Good timing."

"Not my best, but I try."

Vail investigated the hotel room. He saw no one inside. He gazed his eyes toward Donovan while pointing into the room. Donovan looked back into the room and turned to Vail.

"Looking for something?"

"I thought you said Belinda was here?"

"She's at her home." Donovan said. "She will meet with us in the morning. In the meantime, you and I need to discuss this case."

"Sure thing."

Vail entered the hotel room and Donovan followed. Inside, they sat at the coffee table. Atop the table were files Donovan had brought with him. The same documents he emailed to Vail to begin with. Donovan had passed Vail a bottle of beer and Vail drank.

"Plague doctors?" Donovan asked with confusion.

"I saw them at every location the sins had come across. They just stood there. Staring. I taunted one."

"Sounds like something you'll do."

"What would you do if you had a plague doctor staring down at you from across the area?"

"Where did the doctor go?"

"Not sure. I walked away afterwards. Warned it if it followed me it would end up in a far worse place."

"What is your conclusion so far?"

"These areas are connected. The sins aren't traveling by themselves. It's as if they're merged into one. Like they've become an entity."

"You believe the sins have become a living entity? Your presumption I'm assuming?"

"It would explain this more clearly. Besides, the only way for the sins to have merged into an entity, it would need to be brought together by someone of a darker power."

"What of that demon you encountered at Black Raven Hotel? Could he be responsible for this?"

"Wouldn't surprise me. However, he was keen on something else. Regarding myself and others like me in the field."

"How would it know of your future to start with? Demons aren't that intelligent when it comes to one's future. The past they're aware of."

"That demon was more powerful than our usual demons. This one claimed to be a lieutenant demon who worked for somebody called Dagor The Soul Eater."

"The Soul Eater?" Donovan jumped. "He hasn't been seen since the Middle Ages."

"Well, if his lieutenant is bumping around the world, he mustn't be hidden anymore."

"Your words are true." Donovan nodded. "Well, once we meet Belinda tomorrow, she'll tag along with us on this case."

"No offense, but, why is she interested in this case? I'm sure she has plenty of cases in this city."

"She wanted this case to work with you again. Though, not as I expect it to be. We're not going to Poveglia this time."

"Noted." Vail stood up from the table. "I'm going to get myself a room in this place. I'll speak to you in the morning."

"Sure thing, Travis. Good night."

"Same to you." Vail left Donovan's hotel room.

While Vail had obtained his own room, he walked down the hallway toward the room. Before he could put the key in, Vail spotted another plague doctor standing at the end of the hall. Cloaked in darkness. Yet, its' beak was glowing. Vail sighed.

"You choose to do this now?" Vail asked. "I would like some kind of answer here."

The doctor kept still. Vail shook his head and rubbed his hands together.

'Guess I'll have to make you."

Vail moved with haste toward the doctor and once he reached him, the doctor had vanished into a thin dark mist. Vail searched the surroundings and found nothing.

"This nonsense is something else."

Vail returned to his room and unlocked the door. He entered and went to sleep.

III

<u>WHAT CAME BETWEEN</u>

The following morning, Travis Vain and Galen Donovan entered a café and inside sitting was Belinda Grazio. They noticed, and Vail only sighed as they approached the table and sat down.

"I know." Belinda said. "You're thrilled to see me again."

"I know why you're here." Vail said. "Besides, that's not why I'm here."

"She's here to assist us on this case."

"I'm aware. So, let's get to it shall we."

"Fair enough." Donovan said. "We need your skills to help us solve this case around the first sins."

"The first sins? That's your case?"

"Can you help us is the question." Vail pointed out. "Can you?"

"I can help. Only if I can come along with the two of you."

"She would do this." Vail said.

"You can."

"*Prego.*" Belinda said. "Glad we can work together again."

"I'm sure you are." Vail said. "Now, can we discuss this case?"

"Yeah. What do you mean by the 'first sins'?" Belinda asked.

"Travis can give you the details. It is his case after all."

"Sure thing. I've come across a number of plague doctors recently and all pf them have some sort of connection to the first sins."

"Like all of them?"

"Yes."

"And you want to find out where these doctors are going and who could be leading them?"

"Precisely. Which is why Galen decided to speak to you. Believing you could be of service to solving this obscure case."

"Well, I can be of service."

"Excellent. Help us and you can go on your way." Vail said.

"What is the plan for today?"

"Since I was visited by a plague doctor last night, I figured we make a trip back to the hotel and search the area. Perhaps, the quiet doctor left something for us to find."

"Well then, I will gather my things and meet you there."

Vail nodded as Belinda hugged Donovan and left the café. Vail turned to Galen, shaking his head.

"Is it always going to be like this with the two of you?" Donovan asked.

"As long as she focuses on the mission, everything will run smoothly."

"And if not?"

"Then, we will have problems. Delays. Something this job doesn't require us to have."

Vail and Donovan left the café and as they walked down the sidewalk, they stumbled across a pair of street preachers. Dressed in bright colors with the menorah and the Star of David on their clothing. They carried with them signs and a chart, detailing locations of the earth. Vail approached them, glancing at the chart.

"And what is this?"

"What do you think, Esau." The preacher said.

"Heh, Esau now." Vail uttered. "Is that what you just called me?"

"Esau is the white man. You are the Devil!" The Preacher yelled.

"Me the Devil? Look here, fellow, the only one of us who's truly the Devil is you and your gang of deceivers."

"Deceivers?! Read the Word, Esau!"

The Preacher looked, seeing Donovan approaching them next to Vail. The Preacher's eyes glanced back and forth between Vail and Galen.

"My brother, you can't be hanging around with the enemy."

"The enemy? This man is my friend."

"You can't be friends with Esau, my brother. Look at this chart right here."

Donovan looked at the chart and nodded. Facing the preacher and his brothers-in-arms.

"I have a solution to the problem. Mind if I speak it to you?"

"Yes sir."

"If the white man is truly Esau, then he is your brother."

"What do you mean by that?"

"Esau was born from Isaac's loins. Thereby, Esau is in fact a

Hebrew."

"That's not what we're discussing, my brother. The white man is the Devil and the white man is Esau."

"Then, if Esau is the white man and the white man is the Devil, you should get busy at casting the Devil out of him. Free him from the demonic troubles."

The preacher stepped back, grabbing a hold of the Bible in hand. He shook his head.

"We can't help those who's minds have been wiped by the white man. We can't. You're a lost cause, my brother. I am deeply sorry. But, I hope *Yahawashi* has mercy on you and grants you entrance when he returns."

"As do I." Donovan said.

"Heh." Vail chuckled. "Hmm."

The two walked away as the preacher continued his preaching. They turned, entering an alleyway. Vail laughed, and Donovan shook his head.

"Didn't think they would be here." Vail said.

"They're growing. Besides, it's part of the endgame."

"As are many things happening today."

From there, smoke arose from the ground, startling the two. A thick black smoke.

"What is this?" Donovan asked.

"I know who it is."

From the smoke came Kamagrauto, the lieutenant demon. Cloaked in its robe and hood. Its eyes visible from the shadow and its horns spiked out. Kamagrauto levitated over the smoke. His legs could not be seen.

"Travis Vail. Galen Donovan. How intriguing it is to find you both here."

"Is that the demon you talked about?" Donovan asked.

"Yeah. That's him."

Kamagrauto glanced at Vail and Donovan. Its hands held together with his long, sharp, and dirty claws.

"Alright, what do you want?" Vail asked.

"To warn you of your current mission. You will not succeed."

"Is that so?"

"Your future depends on this case and I already know, you will fail. The first sins alone are far too vast for Travis Vail to solve on his own. You need guidance. Guidance from the other side and I can provide such."

"I understand your nobility. But, me and Galen have this under control."

"Oh, you do?" Kamagrauto gestured. "Then, I will be watching your every move and when you desire my aid and you will, I will make myself known unto you and those who will be at your side when the moment comes."

"What moment?" Vail asked.

"You will know. You will know."

Kamagrauto vanished into the smoke by falling. The darkness cleared from the alleyway and there was nothing remaining.

"That demon is noble?" Donovan asked.

"He has honor. I know. Strange for a demon to possess such a moral trait."

"Well, there are things not even we can comprehend."

"True. But, someday, I hope we can. Right now, we need to go and meet Belinda."

Making their return to the hotel, Belinda waited for them. She saw the looks on their faces.

"What happened?"

"We came across a demon." Donovan said.

"Or the demon came to us." Vail added.

"What kind of demon?"

"The lieutenant kind."

"That's not making any sense, Travis."

"I'm afraid it is true, Belinda. It's the same demon Travis met at the Black raven Hotel some time ago."

"Kamagrauto? Here?"

"Oh, you know his name." Vail chuckled.

"I thought you were only seeing things. I didn't expect him to exist."

"Well, lass, he exists and trust me, he's not one you would like to meet. Ask Galen of the encounter."

Donovan looked to Belinda and shook his head.

"Kamagrauto is not the typical demons we face. He is something far more ancient and we could feel his power."

"But, do not fret. He offered to help us."

"I hope you refused."

"Not the slightest. He told me whenever I needed his help involving this case, which he is aware of. So, I assume there are others in the spirit world who are familiar with this and aren't giving us any help. Kamagrauto told me to call on him if I needed his aid."

"But, you won't. we'll solve the first sins together."

"True. But, then again, stranger things have happened in this line of work."

Vail walked to the hotel room door.

"I'm going to return to my room and get ready for the work we have to do. I won't be long."

Vail left the room. Belinda turned to Donovan with uncertainty expressing from her face. Galen knew it and sat down.

"What's with him?"

"What do you mean? That's the way he works. Travis is a very different kind of occult detective."

"Yeah. Not one I would assume to have help from a demon. An ancient one at that."

"Why don't you go and talk to him. See what he tells you."

"He already doesn't want me here."

"And that is more reason for you to talk to him. Get through to him. I know it's possible."

"How so?"

"Because I am the one who trained him in this field. His mentor in a way. Anyway, go and speak with him. It'll give us enough time to prepare to find these plague doctors."

Belinda approached Vail's hotel room door and immediately the door opened. Vail stared at Belinda and she did the same. No words.

"What do you want?" Vail asked.

"Can we talk? For just a second."

Vail sighed as he allowed Belinda into his room. Shutting the door behind, Belinda stood, and Vail walked over to the table and sat down. He gestured his hand toward the other seat. Belinda sat with him.

"What?"

"What's with you?"

"How do you mean?"

"I mean your demeanor, your attitude. What's the problem?"

"There's plague doctors roaming around with the first sins on their back. I have to find out who's causing this and way."

"That's not what I'm talking about."

"Then I'm confused."

Belinda sighed.

"Why couldn't it have worked between us, Travis? Why didn't you bother to give it a chance?"

"You are not seriously asking me about relationship details right now."

"I am."

"Women always want to talk."

"Only if the men would listen to our words."

"I'm not trying to build up bitterness in my heart, lass. Besides that, I've told you before. A relationship with me won't work."

"Why not?"

"Because when I was young, I was visited by an angel. The angel warned me not to get married. Otherwise, tragedy would follow. Now, I see what the angel meant. Me traveling on this road of life. Dealing with the supernatural daily. Heh, if I did have a wife, she would've most likely divorced me or been killed in the process."

"But, there's always a way."

"Even though you're in this line of work, tragedy still strikes. The fact of Kamagrauto confronting me, proves the angel's point."

"Well, did this angel have a name?"

"He did."

"What was it?"

"Hmm. Michael."

"As in Michael the Archangel."

"Correct. Funny enough, he's been overseeing my activities since I was a little boy. No worries. However, I am keen on the fact he hasn't intervened with my confrontations with Kamagrauto. Maybe time will tell this course."

Vail sighed. Standing up from the chair, he grabbed his coat from the back of the chair, putting it on.

"Now, let's continue this case of ours."

IV

<u>WHAT CAME WITHIN</u>

Vail and Belinda met with Galen, who found the two of them together somewhat odd, but never the case. They moved forward with the case and after studying the trail of the plague doctor that Vail saw, a clue was given. A name connected to a series of plague doctor sightings. Belinda had the name.

"What is it?" Vail asked.

"Here's the name of the recent plague doctor sightings. All from witnesses who've seen the doctors and later a man would come and visit them. Asking about the doctors before they ever went public with a concern."

"The man's name." Donovan said. "What was it?"

"Timothy Ellis."

"Timothy Ellis. I've never heard of him before."

"I have." Vail said. "It's familiar to my ears."

"What do you know of this man, Travis?"

"He's deeply into the spiritual arts. Mystic stuff as well. But, in the occult circles, he doesn't go by that name. he is known and referred to as Balthazar."

"Is this the mage Balthazar a few have talked about?"

"It is. Balthazar is a mage. A powerful one. Took the name from the biblical magi. Cloaked in his dark-orange hood and robe, he gained power from a deep malevolent force. One of which I am unknown to. But, in time I will find out."

"So, where is Balthazar?" Belinda asked.

"New York City." Vail said. "Which means we have some traveling to do and in little time."

"Yeah, but how long before he finds out we're on to him?"

Vail turned and noticed a shadow hovering in the distance. He stared, and it revealed its eyes.

"Not long." Vail said, staring at the shadow.

"What is it?" Belinda said, turning to also see the shadow.

"What is that?" Donovan asked.

"Balthazar sent him." Vail said. "He already knows."

Vail ran after the shadow without haste.

"Where are you going?!" Belinda yelled.

"I'm going to see what this spirit knows!" Vail answered. "Don't follow me!"

Belinda went to follow, and Donovan held her back.

"Travis can handle himself."

"That's not what I'm worried about."

Vail chased the shadow, leaving Belinda and Donovan behind. The shadow brought Vail to a spot which was filthy, and the ground was covered in feces and vomit.

"Smells like shit." Vail uttered.

From its appearance, Vail knew it was a spot for homeless people.

"Show yourself, spirit." Vail yelled.

"In front of him, the shadow appeared. Yet, no fear within it as it morphed into physical form. It resembled a young man, yet he was covered in blood, and chewed on swine's flesh. Vail smirked.

"The hell have we got here. A sin entity."

"Balthazar will have your soul." The entity uttered.

"I think not."

Vail tossed a handful of salt on the entity, startling it. There, Vail began to recite a chant, commanding for the entity to be loosed from Balthazar's hold and to return into the void. The entity was powerful enough to break Vail's chant, forcefully shoving him to the brick wall behind him. Vail fell to the ground and quickly, Kamagrauto arose from the pavement, snatching the entity by the throat and biting it, ripping off its astral head as the body returned to shadow form and fell. Evaporating into thin air.

"I'm not understanding any of this." Vail said.

"You have a higher calling, Travis Vail and I will not allow anyone to turn you away from your cause."

"You know about Balthazar? And how he's behind these plague doctors scaring folks."

"Balthazar has risen up the first sins. Yes. But, there is another spirit lurking the world. One far more powerful than Balthazar and is on the run from another soul as we speak."

"I wish that particular soul the best in his endeavors. Could use the bit of the help every now and then. How come you didn't tell me all this before I went further?"

"I know many things. Things even the smartest man would tremble at the sound."

"Good thing, I'm not the smartest man. I'm just an exorcist."

"One with a higher purpose."

"Then, why don't you just travel onto New York City and stop Balthazar for me? That way, I can focus more on this 'higher purpose'."

'Because it is not my duty to finish your work. You started this case, you must finish it."

Vail chuckled.

"I'll be. You know your kind are some slick sons of bitches."

"Do not compare me to the common demons you've slain."

"I'm not." Vail asked. "But, you really are a strange demon, lad."

"I am not like those demons. I am Kamagrauto. Kamagrauto."

Kamagrauto vanished into the black smoke as before. Vail shrugged himself and scoffed.

V

<u>WHAT CAME ABOUT</u>

Vail returned to Belinda and Galen, who saw his tiredness and often slackly behavior after things have arisen. They approached him with concern and he only smiled.

"What happened to the shadow?" Donovan asked.

"It was taken care of."

"How?" Belinda wondered.

"Kamagrauto killed it."

"The demon Kamagrauto?"

"Yes, Galen. The same demon we met in the alleyway. I confronted the damn thing. By the way, the shadow was a sin entity."

"That can't be so?" Donovan said. "there hasn't been one of them since the World Wars."

"And yet, here it is and not out of curiously either. Balthazar conjured it up."

"What happened to the spirit, Travis?" Belinda asked.

"I nearly came close to casting it away, but it possessed a power that outweigh my voice and tossed me against the wall.

After that, Kamagrauto appeared and decapitated the spirit. Good for me."

"The demon helped you?" Donovan asked. "It killed the spirit right in front of your eyes?"

"Yes. Afterwards we spoke, and he revealed to me he's been aware of this whole case the entire time. I scoffed and wondered how come he couldn't do the work for us. Said it wasn't in his purpose. However, Balthazar is the one behind all of this and there's another sin spirit roaming the earth. But, Kamagrauto confirmed to me that another individual is chasing that spirit right now. So, hopefully we won't have too much work on our hands."

"So, what is our current objective?" Belinda asked.

"Galen, call Colton, tell him to meet us in New York. We need to confront Balthazar now and fast before more of his little ideas manifest into reality."

Vail, Belinda, and Donovan made their travels and arrived in New York City. Prepared to meet Balthazar. Wherever he may reside.

VI

<u>WHAT CAME TO BE</u>

Vail, Belinda, and Donovan stood in Times Square. Seeing the crowds go by, walking about their business. Galen shook his head in shame.

"They're just coming and going."

"It's their nature, Galen. Besides, it proves we're not the ones trapped in Pop Culture and materialism."

"Now, where will Colton be?" Belinda asked.

"He should be around here somewhere."

Vail looked out, not seeing his ally. Later, he turned his head and from there, he managed to get a glance at Colton. He pointed.

"He's coming this way."

Colton Levi approached them and shook hands. Standing in the middle of Times Square mind you amid the roaming crowds.

"Good to see you." Vail said. "Now, why did you want us to meet you out here?"

"Because, the guy you're looking for oftentimes roams through here."

"Are you sure?"

"Plague doctors are seen continually here. It's looked at as just a cosplay show."

"Point us in the direction." Vail said.

They followed Colton through the Square, moving past the crowds. There, Vail and Galen noticed a group of street preachers, yelling at all the white men in the crowds. Vail scoffed as the argument escalated to a brawl.

"They're everywhere."

"It's part of the times, Travis." Donovan said.

"True one."

Colton had led them into a spot where they set shops. He pointed toward the spot which had a crescent moon carved on the door.

"Is this the spot?" Belinda asked.

"It certainly is." Vail confirmed. "Let's see what's inside."

They entered the shop and quickly, surrounded by plague doctors. They raised up their guards as the doctors stood quirt and still.

"Oh, this is the place." Vail said.

The doctors approached them and suddenly, took steps back. Moving in a fashioned line on each side, leading them further into the shop down a hallway. They walked down the hallway and they reached a room. In the room were images of occult symbols, sacrifices, and spells. A pentagram was carved into the wooden floor. Vail stepped forward, seeing a hooded man crouched down at the fire.

"Stand up, you're embarrassing yourself here." Vail said.

The hooded man stood up, removing his hood. Revealing

himself to be Balthazar. Vail smiled. Pointing.

"You son of a bitch!" Vail laughed.

"Travis Vail. The Spirit-Seeker."

"In the flesh."

"I figured you would come."

"Had not choice, lad. I've come to stop your doings. Raising up plague doctors and spirits. The shit has to stop."

"It will not cease until my work is complete."

"Your work is done. Just let it all go. Quit working for the enemy and just retire."

Balthazar raised his hands, shoving Belinda, Galen, and Colton to the floor. Holding them in place with a sort of spiritual bind. Only he and Vail remained standing.

"Why are you doing this?"

"Because I have a master to praise. One who granted me these gifts. I must serve him with all my might."

"Then, your master has to deal with me. And others out there."

"My master's coming was already thwarted by someone. I will not allow the Cryptic Zone to remain shut. He will rise."

"No, he won't."

"And what will you do when he rises and comes for you?"

"Don't all malevolent forces come for me? It's my job to piss your kind off."

"How about a deal."

"A what now?"

"A deal. You leave me to my work and I let your friends live."

"Um, deal declined. However, I can offer you a deal."

"Like so?"

"Let my friends go or find yourself entering Hell a little early than you expected."

"You cannot kill me." Balthazar declared. "No man can murder me!"

"I'm not going to murder you. I'm simply going to offer you a trip. Besides, best you deal with me and not Kamagrauto."

Balthazar froze. His eyes went wider.

"Kamagrauto?" Balthazar asked.

"Yes. You know, lieutenant demon. Works for Dagor the Soul Eater. That kind of guy. He knows of your work by the way. Told me of it. Raising the first sins and all. Plague doctors and such. He knows. And if he knows, who's the say the others know as well."

Balthazar shook, dropping the hold on Belinda, Galen, and Colton. Vail smirked.

"They will not have me." Balthazar said. "My master will protect me!"

"Then, let's see him protect you from this."

Vail raised up his hand, shoving Balthazar down. He began to chant and before he could start, a whirlwind of blue flames surrounded Balthazar. Taking him away. The room was silent. Galen approached the spot. Belinda and Colton were confused.

"The hell just happened?" Colton asked.

"His master took him." Vail said.

"What of the first sins?" Belinda asked. "What of the doctors?"

"We'll see if they still stand." Donovan said.

They returned to the entrance, discovering the doctors are gone. Vail knew Balthazar's fear had driven the doctors and the first sins away. He smirked as they left the shop. The case was done. Yet, Balthazar was somewhere in the world. Possibly in other realms of existence. Vail knew he would see him again down the road.

With everyone returning to their proper places, Vail sat inside his own domain, researching more on the sin entity Kamagrauto mentioned in their conversation. There, Vail discovered there's an ancient power had risen, which is the cause for the sin entity's presence.

"In my line of work, things happen for the worst. Usually the better."

He knew the power was far too great for himself to face. By that standard, Vail went to visit a friend. A friend in Washington D.C.

THE DEVILHUNTER: UNSEEN WORSHIP

I

A CROWDED AFFAIR

Strange worshippers rushed into an empty church during the night. Carrying books, candles, staves, and many other objects. Laying them around in a circle. They were cloaked in black, scarlet, and violet robes and hoods. One of the black hoods lit a fire in the circle of the objects. There were a dozen worshippers in the church as they went down on their knees and began to pray.

"Oh, Great Lord. We call upon your name this night. To guide us to your magic's and to your mysteries. Reveal unto us your truths and your words. Grant us the power we so crave. For it is our sole duty to serve you."

Immediately, the church doors bolted open, revealing a man of an Eastern descent. He entered the church, raising up a shotgun and began shooting at the worshippers. The ran throughout the church as he fired at them. Killing them with every shot. He took a moment to reload the weapon and one of the hooded ones attacked him from behind. Stumbling, he caught himself and faced the attacker.

"Tell me." The man said. "Where is your lord?"

"For he is here. He is everywhere."

"You have me all wrong. He's not with you. You're speaking of someone else. Someone from another realm."

"You know." The hooded one said. "Then, our task is complete."

"What do you mean?"

"A sacrifice. A blood sacrifice had to be made of our lives and you've delivered it to our master. Who is near."

"Who is your master? Tell me?"

"***Sit laus Festinatio.***" The hooded one said before the man blew his head off.

The man sighed. He searched the church, only to find the objects the hooded ones brought in and the circle of fire. Pouring dirt from the outside atop the fire to put it out, he discovered a pentagram was carved into the wooden floor and the fire was lit above it. He scoffed.

"I knew you were the ones."

This man is Gabriel Abraham. Known to the supernatural community as Abraham The Devil Hunter or simply The Devilhunter. Abraham walked out of the church with the ringing voice of the hooded one's words. Spoken in Latin. Abraham knew what he said and what he told him was, "*Praise Hastur.*"

Abraham returned to his facility, called the Revelation Center. Inside, he entered his office, where could be seen the document containing the mystery of the Mutant-Thing, and his writings of the encounter with Travis Vail, Cinderella, and The Swordman. Moving those aside, he grabbed an old history book from the shelf and sat down to read. There, flipping through the pages, he came across a page dedicated to a ancient demon known as Hastur.

"Why bring you here?" Abraham questioned. "A blood sacrifice he said."

Knocking came from the front door. Abraham heard it and walked over. Opening the door to reveal a man and a woman. They were startled as the door opened, seeing Abraham with the book in hand. The man was in his late 20s. A handsome one, dressed in slacks and a buttoned shirt with his sleeves up. The young woman was in mid 20s, an modest looking woman in jeans and a low-cut shirt. she wore little makeup, which intrigued Abraham.

"Are you Gabriel Abraham?" The woman asked. "The Gabriel Abraham?"

"Who's asking?"

"You might not remember me." The young man said.

"Tell me your name." Abraham said.

"Evan Wyatt. We've spoken once before concerning science and religion. Before your tragedy."

"Oh. Well, it's been a very long time."

"It has, sir."

"And who is this woman accompanying you?"

"Andrea Coralline."

"Ah. Hispanic descent. It truly shows. Yet, the name doesn't fit the credentials of your nation."

"It's what happens when foreigners come and raid your land."

"Duly noted." Abraham chuckled. "Come in."

Evan and Andrea entered the Center, seeing the number of statues and artifacts sitting within its walls. Abraham shut the door and stood toward them, closing the book in hand.

"Tell me why you've come to seek me out."

"There's been some strange activity going on in the world." Andrea said. "Stuff that hasn't been seen for centuries."

"And how do you know of this?"

"I am a paranormal investigator and part-time occult detective."

"Evan, what of yourself?"

"I'm new to all of this. I met Andrea after she rescued me from a group of Satanists. They ganged up on me and I couldn't defend myself."

"Pulled into a world you're not familiar with."

"Yes. Is the reason you're doing all of this because of losing your wife and daughter."

"I know what attacked them that day. Took them away from me and now I have the means to fight back."

"By making sure no one else has the same experience."

"Yes. It is a task I must do."

Abraham walked over to the statue of Baphomet, which sat in the front of the Center, yet it was scarred ad burnt. Appeared to be the case of someone attempting to destroy the statue by any means and failing to do so.

"Why are you here?" Abraham asked again.

"We need your help in stopping these activities."

"There's plenty of occult detectives roaming the world. Why

didn't you contact Dr. Galer Donovan or the Spirit-Seeker? Why me?"

"Because we believe you would be the one to help us and equip us in this life."

"You want me to be your teacher."

"Something like that."

"Then, you have an even bigger concern. I had a group of pupils once. Until we lost a member. Beth Grasslands. A young girl on the verge of presenting the existence of demons to the public. But, she was taken from us and the pupils ran. Never to enter this job again."

"Was she killed?" Evan asked.

"I don't think so. Few of the pupils claimed she vanished into a wormhole. Probably trapped in another dimension or another world. However, she is lost to us. Lost to me and I will not allow such an act happen again to anyone under my wing."

"I'm sorry for your losses." Evan said. "Truly."

"Don't be. Just be certain others will not share in such a tragedy."

"Then, teach us. Help us in this matter."

Abraham sighed. "What are you seeking?"

"We discovered a succubus that lives in this city. We know how to find her, and we need your help in killing her."

"A succubus?" Abraham said. "Intriguing. Besides demons, there's more entering the land of the living."

"What do you mean?" Evan asked.

"I will explain on the way."

Abraham grabbed his coat and approached the door. He

turned back, seeing Andrea and Evan just standing there. Lost for words and movement. Abraham chuckled.

"Are you going to show me where this succubus dwells?"

"Oh, yeah." Andrea said. "Right."

"Of course, sir." Evan said. "Andrea knows better than me."

Leaving the building and entering Abraham's vehicle, dating back to the 1970s, Abraham drove off from the Center.

II

SEDUCTION OF THE HUNTER

"What is your goal once this is all done?" Andrea asked.

"My goal?" Abraham said. "The only goal is to make sure no one else suffers in such a way as I. Besides, I am aware my job will be done once I'm dead."

"How many things have you encountered since you began this role as a demon hunter?" Evan wondered.

"I've come across many strange things. From ghosts, ghouls, demons, myths and legends. Hell, I've met a fairy tale figure and the Mythological Man."

"Never heard of a Mythological Man." Evan said.

"What fairy tale figure did you meet?" Andrea asked. "I'm curious."

"A famous one."

"But, which one? You'll have to be specific with me."

"Glass slippers. Fairy Godmother. You know."

"Oh. That one. So, does she really wear a nice dress and glass slippers?"

"No. Her dress is far from what the stories tell."

Abraham continued to drive, nearing the outskirts of Washington D.C. He looked around, only seeing the wilderness.

"Now, where does this succubus dwell? Where's the location?"

"In these woods." Andrea said. "Truly, she stays there mostly."

"Are you sure?"

"I am. Came across her during a walk."

"You were walking out here? By yourself?"

"Yeah. I wasn't harmed. The succubus wouldn't attack me. I'm a woman."

"Gender doesn't matter to a succubus. Believe me. They will take whatever they can get."

Abraham stopped the car. They exited and walked into the wilderness. Rarely any other vehicles passed by, which he noticed immediately. Walking deeper into the forest, Abraham spotted a shrine. Gesturing his hand toward Andrea and Evan quickly.

"Stop."

"What is that?" Evan asked.

"It's hers. And from where it sits, she's very close."

The trees behind the shrine rustled and from there, arose a woman wearing a blue silk dress, her wavy black hair mixed with the colors of the forest and the dress. Her eyes glistened with the moon as did her red lips.

"You've come." She said. "Beautiful."

"That her?" Abraham asked.

"It is." Andrea said. "She's the one."

Abraham nodded, turning his focus toward the woman.

"What is your name, succubus?"

"Those who damn me call me whole, prostitute, cunt, bitch, and anything else you wish to harm me with. But, those who love me and desire my fruits, they call me Sierra."

"Well then, Sierra. I am Gabriel Abraham. The Devilhunter and I am here to grant you leave from Washington D.C. and its surrounding neighbors."

"Oh. I just came here and I'm not going anywhere."

"What makes you say that?"

"Because, I'm here on orders from someone higher than my rank. Someone who knows what you did to his worshippers in that church."

"You work for Hastur?"

"Does it make you feel unconformable?"

"No. but, it gives me all I need to know about you."

Sierra turned her glance toward Evan. She smiled, gesturing him to come forward. Evan moved toward her without noticing. Andrea looked at him strangely. Unaware of his motive.

"What are you doing?" She asked.

"Evan, fight it!" Abraham yelled. "She's luring you with her power. Don't submit to it."

"Honey, it's all right. I will not hurt him. Only pleasure him in ways the human woman cannot do."

Evan moved closer to the point where Sierra's fingers rubbed his cheek. Abraham moved forward, knocking Evan to the ground. There, he raised up his gun, aimed at Sierra.

"Step back, demon."

"You wouldn't shoot me." Sierra laughed. "I'm only here to give a love unfamiliar to humanity. The love of your dreams. Love that will make even the toughest man wet himself of relief."

"Don't try it." Abraham gestured; gun aimed closely.

Sierra laughed, backing up into the shadow of the forest. As she backed away, her eyes glowed and from there, she jumped out with a screech. Her beautiful face was gone and had transformed into one of a monster. Long, sharp fangs came out of her mouth. She didn't appear human anymore. She was no what she truly is. A demon.

"Andrea, get Evan out of here now!" Abraham yelled, firing at Sierra.

Andrea grabbed Evan and ran out of the forest to the car. Behind them, they could hear the gunshots firing mixed with Sierra's screeching. In the forest, Abraham moved and dodged Sierra's claw swipes. He shot her in the shoulder and hip, but she kept moving. Shaking his head, he kicked her to the ground and stepped on her right leg.

"I'm finishing you off."

Sierra's screech turned into another sound. One of a calling and Abraham knew it. He backed up from her before shooting her in the leg. She couldn't stand up and the screech grew louder. Andrea and Evan were in the car. Andrea turned, seeing Abraham running from the wilderness.

"Take the keys." Abraham said, tossing the keys to Andrea.

"What are you doing?"

"She called some of her friends. I'm going to hold them off."

"You can't."

"I can. Take Evan back to the Center. I will meet you there once I'm done with these things."

"How will you get back?"

"I'll find a way. Now go."

Andrea paused and nodded. Entering the car and driving away. As soon as she went forward, she could see a horde come from the forest. A horde of demons. They rushed toward Abraham and he began to fight them off with his gun, later pulling out a silver sword from his coat. Last thing Andrea could see was Abraham cutting down the demons with the sword as she was more distant from the spot, returning to the Center.

III

ALL FOR ONE

Abraham battled the hordes around him with his gun and sword. Slashing towards any of them who stepped closer. He looked around the area, no sign of Sierra. He figured she remained in the woods to keep herself from further harm. The horde suddenly froze in motion. Abraham was dumbfounded as he walked past them, their eyes did not blink, nor did they breathe. It was as if a switch was turned off within them. Abraham sighed.

"The hell is going on?"

The horde went back into motion, walking backwards into the forest. Abraham slashed the ones closets to them to avoid more entering, however, they did not harm him and as the last one entered the forest, the trees closed together.

"Something's not right about this." Abraham breathed.

Meanwhile, Andrea and Evan returned to the Center, only to find it covered with Worshippers of Hastur. Andrea stopped the car near the entrance and froze. Evan began to wake up from the hit by Abraham and saw the hooded figures surrounding the building.

"Holy shit!" Evan said.

"Damn it!" Andrea responded. "Keep your voice down."

The worshippers stood still. They were chanting Hastur's name. all in motion and quietly. Their hands were to their side and their heads down. Faces couldn't be seen due to the hoods. Andrea and Evan remained still.

"What are we going to do?" Evan asked.

"I'll call Gabriel. Hopefully he's still alive."

"What happened with him?"

"After you succumb to Sierra's charms, Gabriel knocked you out to keep her from killing you. There, a horde of Hastur's kind came out of the forest. Gabriel fought them off for me to get us out of there."

Andrea dialed on her cell phone and it rang. Across the city, Abraham was walking down the sidewalk, leaving the forest. He can feel his phone vibrating in his jacket, he took it out.

"Yes."

"Good, you're still alive. I have some news to tell you."

"Same here." Abraham said. "What's yours?"

"Hastur's worshippers are at the Center."

"Seriously?"

"Yes."

Evan tapped her, pointing to the worshippers, she gazed as she saw them entering the Center.

"Um, Abraham, they're entering the Center."

"Who left a door open?"

"No one. It looks like they're being guided in. Someone else is inside."

"Hastur." Abraham uttered. "I'm on my way. Stay put!"

Abraham hung up and started running. Andrea and Evan remained in the car. Once the worshippers were in, they exited Abraham's car and crept up to the windows. There, they could see who else was inside and it was Hastur himself. Standing in the spot where the Baphomet statue was once placed.

"I didn't know he looked like that." Evan said.

"Me either."

Hastur's appearance was of a full demon. Had to be around ten or twelve feet in height. He had wings on his back, he wore a tunic and he had ram horns on his head. His eyes were red as blood and his feet resembled goat's hooves.

"What do we do?" Evan asked. "He's too strong for us to take on ourselves."

"We wait on Gabriel."

"Are you sure he's coming?"

"I'm positive."

IV

<u>FALLEN'S WAY</u>

Within the Center, Hastur's worshippers began to bow down to him. He stood tall, savoring the scenery. Andrea and Evan continued to watch through the window from the outside. Abraham was inching closer to the Center as he continued moving.

"This place is covered with symbolism." Hastur said with a deep voice. "A haven for my enemies."

"What are we going to do?" Evan asked.

"We wait here for Gabriel to come."

"What if Hastur leaves before he makes his way back?"

"I don't know. But, I have something in mind."

"Like what?"

"It may be stupid. However, I believe it's worth a shot."

"Tell me what it is."

The doors bolted open and Andrea and Evan entered with weapons in their hand. The worshippers all turned their heads toward them at the same time. Hastur glared at them with a smirk.

"This part of your plan?" Evan uttered.

"Not really." Andrea said. "But, we're inside."

Who are you two?" Hastur asked. "You're not native to this place."

"How do you know?" Andrea asked.

"Your scent comes from another place. Another field. This building isn't your home. It's someone else's"

"He's on his way here." Evan said. "He's the one who took out your worshippers in that abandoned church."

Hastur took a step forward toward Andrea and Evan. They stood their ground, yet, Evan took one step back out of fear of the tall demon.

"What is his name?"

"My name is Gabriel Abraham." Came a voice from the entrance.

Hastur looked, along with Andrea and Evan. Abraham stood at the door and behind him, a blue car had vanished from the entrance. Driving away with speed.

"How did you get back?" Andrea asked.

"Someone gave me a ride."

"You killed my worshippers?" Hastur asked.

"Yes." Abraham replied. "Your kind are a cancer to the world. I am one of the few who is determined to put you back in your place."

"A demon hunter." Hastur scoffed. "I've met many throughout the eons of this creation."

"Abraham raised up his silver sword. Pointing it toward the demon.

"Let's see who survives this day."

"I'm not here to kill you, demon hunter." Hastur said. "I've come to mark my territory for the coming war."

"What war?" Andrea asked.

"The war of the heavens. This city is only one of the spots upon the earth that will suffer from its cause. You've chosen a bad place to dwell, demon hunter."

"I'll take my chances."

Abraham rushed over, swiping the sword against Hastur's leg. The burning flowed through him as he roared in pain. The worshippers rose up from the floor, coming towards Abraham. Hastur extended his hand, stopping them. He stared at Abraham.

"No battle is worth much bloodshed and tragedy this day. Yet, I give you this warning. I will return soon and when I do, it will be our battle. One of us will not live to tell the story."

"I intend on waiting and I will win."

Hastur grinned and warped into a fiery wormhole, sucking in the worshippers as well, including the Baphomet statue. The wormhole shut. Evan approached its spot and sighed.

"So, can we stay?" Andrea asked. "You can teach us as we asked."

"Fine." Abraham said. "I'll teach you."

Sometime later, while Abraham worked in his office, a knock came from the door. Abraham rose up to answer it and as he stood up, he saw a man standing at the office door. Wearing all black besides a white buttoned shirt. The man had his hands in his coat pocket. Abraham was staring at Travis Vail, the Spirit-Seeker.

"Too soon." Vail said with a grin.

THE MAN CALLED FABLE: THE MAGE AND THE CON

I

WANT TO HAVE A <u>CONVERSATION?</u>

In the rift between the natural world and the magical realm, Pandora, a cloaked and hooded woman powerful within magic has summoned Kurt Wesker, who's known in the magic realm as The Man Called Fable. Fable, decked out in his brown duster coat, slacks, boots, and open-buttoned shirt stares at Pandora with confusion. His scruffy hair and facial hair moved with the brushing of the wind between the rift. The rift was warped with many colors, flowing up and down and around. Looked as if one could be hallucinating.

"You know why I summoned you." Pandora said.

"I'm familiar with the setting and all, but, I was in the middle of a card game. I had it won."

"Meaning you would lead the magical creatures out into the open as you've done before?"

"Not exactly. See, what happened that day was not my fault. Just a troll and his friends having some emotional issues. That's all."

"Then, what happened to Erkac the satyr was just a coincidence?"

Fable shrugged his shoulders and cocked his head with a smile.

"He wanted to go for a job. I spoke him a word and he took off. Exercise helps even the satyr kind."

"Never mind the past, Fable. I have called you because of a dire concern."

"What concern would have me involved?"

"Your thoughtless actions, moving between the natural and magical realms has sent out tears between the realms. Due to that, we've discovered an entity of the magical realm has returned and is looking to make the natural world his own."

"Does this guy have a name? Something that I can keep track of?"

"His name, we do not know."

Fable approached Pandora, looking her in the eyes. Her glowing warped eyes. They warped as the walls around them.

"No name?" Fable asked. "Hmm. I'll figure something out. You won't like it, but it will be done."

Fable walked toward the rift, preparing his way out.

"Tread carefully, Fable." Pandora commanded. "For this foe could be anywhere at any time."

Fable turned to Pandora and grinned.

"I'll be fine." Fable said as he walked through the rift, vanishing from Pandora's eyes.

Back in the natural world, Denise Kira, a reporter has been tracking down evidence of many cases since the rise of the heroes across the world. Kira searched the city of Manchester for any heroes of its own. After three months of searching, she's found one. In Fable himself.

II

GREETING A CON ARTIST WITHOUT MAGIC

During the night in Manchester, Fable entered a peculiar bar. One in the middle of the city. A bar full of magical creatures. As he stepped in, a troll sitting at a table in the center, waved his hand in the air.

"You've shown up."

"Of course, I would." Fable said. "Why wouldn't I?"

Fable went and sat at the table. Being surrounded by more trolls and a goblin. Fable smirks at the young woman at the bar, sipping her drink. The troll sitting down shook his head in disgust.

"Your kind have that problem deeply rooted."

"What problem?"

"The deep attraction for the opposite sex. It clouds your judgment."

"You believe that doll at the bar will cloud my chances of winning tonight?"

"Absolutely. Because I will leave here the winner and a richer man."

"Em. I wouldn't go around calling yourself a man. You're a troll, dude."

"You get the fucking point!"

"Sure, man. Sure. Figure of speech. I get it."

They began to play. Gaining a larger crowd by every hit. The bar door opened and Denise entered. She cannot believe what she is seeing, a place full of magic beings. She walked past satyrs, elves, fairies, and she looked ahead, seeing the crowd surrounding Fable and the troll during their card game.

"It's him." She said to herself.

Fable and the troll continued their game of cards. Rallying on the crowd. Full of beer and cheers. Fable laid on the table, a set of yellow cards with a large red circle in the middle, surrounded by four black circle and a triangle in the center of the circle. A connected double dash was also on the cards. The troll stared at the cards, gazing toward Fable with confusion.

"I've never seen those before."

"There's a rare type. I'll let you have them if you can beat me."

"Then, you've already given them to me."

The troll laid his cards on the table. The crowd startled. Fable looked concerned as the troll laughed. Fable showed a faint grin, placing one of the strange cards on the table. The troll bounced from the table with anger.

"You bastard! You cheated!"

"No." Fable grinned. "I won. Fair play."

"Son of a bitch!" The troll yelled, jumping over to the table, attacking Fable.

The crowds broke the two apart as Fable reached, retrieving the strange cards. Placing them in his duster pocket. Fixing his coat, he raised his hands in the air.

"It's cool, guys. It's cool. I won and now I'm going to leave."

"You better leave, boy." The troll uttered. "Don't think me one like Erkac and his goons."

"Why does everyone know about my situation with Erkac?"

"Shit travels."

"Well played." Fable laughed.

Fable turned to leave, bumping into Denise. He stared at her and she stared back. Their eyes locked onto one another.

"Hello." Fable said.

"Hi." Denise replied.

The two continued to stare until Fable nodded and left the bar. Denise took a moment to take in the scene and she too left the bar. Outside, she looked around, spotting Fable ahead.

"Excuse me!" Denise yelled.

Fable turned around, seeing Denise approaching him.

"What have I done now?" Fable asked.

"Nothing. Nothing at all."

"Then, what do you want?"

"I have to ask. Are you the man they call Fable?"

"Heh. The Man Called Fable. Nice ring to it. Um, what do you think? Do I look like The Man Called Fable?"

"I don't know. I've never seen him before. But, back in the bar, your actions and your dress suits what I've read about him."

"Wait, read? Where?"

"There's many sightings concerning Fable." Denise said.

"People are writing about me?"

"So, you are Fable."

"Spotted. Yes, I am Fable. The Man Called Fable."

"Then, the rift between our world and the magical realm is true."

"How do you know so much about this world and the magic realm?"

"I've done a lot of studying."

"Like, how much studying? Did you get any sleep from all of this discovery? A revelation deprived you of sleep?"

"One thing I must ask, have you ever considered traveling to London to assist their vigilante?"

"What vigilante?"

"The woman."

"Oh. We both know fairy tale figures do not exist."

"Then, why have I just left a bar where you were fighting a troll. A bar surrounded by magical creatures."

Fable paused. He nodded with a wink.

"The world isn't what the general public believes it to be."

"Please, I want to know more about this magical realm. What lies in it? How much of magic are we to know is true?"

"Enough to live without a crisis."

"I have more questions for you, Fable."

"Then, you know where to find me." Fable smiled, walking away.

Fable turned a corner with a smile on his face. As he turned, Pandora was waiting for him, startling him.

"Don't do that."

"What were you doing?"

"What do you mean? I wanted to have some fun at the bar. Probably a little too much fun."

"I'm not talking about your little scuffle in the bar."

"Then, I'm lost."

"Speaking with a human woman concerning their world and the magic realm."

"She already knew."

"Yet, you were present for her to continue asking questions. She already knew of your existence."

"About that. How did she know?"

"Erkac."

Fable sighed. "You can't be serious."

"It is true."

"That little incident couldn't have traveled such far lengths."

"Well, it did. Your actions are causing much more harm than good."

"Is that what the growing power is all about? My actions? Speaking of which, what of this force you warned me about?"

"We've discovered his name."

"That's a start. What is it, Pandora? The name."

"Emblem."

"Sounds like a necklace."

"This is no joking matter. Emblem is a powerful magician. A wizard from the ancient past. He has returned with malevolent intentions in mind. As for now, do not speak with those outside the magical realm. We don't need any more innocent lives in danger."

Fable nodded.

"I understand."

"I will speak to you soon."

Pandora vanished in a rift between the worlds. Fable stood there and nodded.

"Ok." Fable walked off.

Behind him, Denise stood by the corner of the building. She has seen and heard everything.

"What the fuck?"

III

<u>SURROUNDED BY FOUR CORNERS</u>

Fable returned to his home, a shack in the Cheshire Plain. Upon opening the door, Fable stopped and stared, seeing four hooded individuals standing in his home. Dressed in gold-and-white robes. Their faces hidden by the hoods. Fable entered the home, slamming the door.

"Figured you guys would show up."

One of the hooded ones approached Fable slowly, standing before him with a greater height.

"You guys are much taller than I originally remember."

"Pandora has spoken to you about Emblem?"

"Yes. She told me about the guy. I haven't seen him."

"But, you will assist us in stopping him from gaining strength from the rift."

"Yeah. About that." Fable said, walking toward the kitchen. "This whole thing isn't part of my job. Remember, I'm a con artist. One who touts magic as his weapon."

"We know of your persona here in the physical realm. But, what shall you do when the realms merge by Emblem's growing

87

power?"

"Look, four hoods, I have been doing this life since I was a lad, now, I am positive there are others out there who know about the magic realm that can assist you in taking out this Emblem guy. Not me."

"Emblem is already on this plane. His powers are growing and very soon, he will warp this reality and merge in with the magic realm. Afterwards, all of life will be in his hand."

Fable grabbed a beer bottle from the refrigerator, approaching the hooded one. He opened the bottle and took a sip with a grin on his face.

"Then, you don't need me."

The hooded one turned toward his brethren as they stood around Fable. He glanced around, seeing the four standing and staring at him. Fable took another sip of the beer and held it out.

"You guys want a beer or something?"

"Soon, you will understand there is more consequences to this world than you've been led to believe."

"I'll take my chances."

The four vanished through a sudden rift. Leaving Fable's home. He drank the beer and sighed.

"A visit from the Hidden Four is always a means for another drink."

Denise arrived at her apartment, shutting the door and turning on the light. Putting down her bag, she turned around, only to find Pandora standing in her apartment. She started to yell, but, Pandora waved her hand, muting the sound of the scream.

"Keep quiet." Pandora commanded.

Denise nodded, Pandora removed the mute from her mouth. Denise moved over slowly, towards the table as Pandora continued to stand in place.

"I saw you. Speaking with Fable near the bar."

"I figured you did. Which is why I'm here in your domain."

"What do you want with me?"

"I have come to warn you."

"Warn me of what?"

"Fable."

"What about him?"

"He's a dangerous man."

"He didn't seem so bad during our conversation."

"The more you interact with him, the more the magical realm learns of your existence and your knowledge of its presence. I am giving you a chance to save your life before you place it into further harm."

"So, it's all real." Denise breathed. "All of it. The rift. Fable's magic knowledge. Placing within this world where the magical creatures dwell. It's all true."

"Yes, and it is for the better you do not entertain the idea of entering such a world. Your life among the humans is enough for one such as yourself."

"But, there is so much to learn about the magical realm. How it was formed. Who formed it and why does it exist? Questions much of the world should truly know."

"The rising heroes have already gained your world's attention. They do not need more details into the true reality of this existence. For it may bring damnation into your lives and eventually take you away from it."

Denise nodded with confusion.

"I don't get this. Why keep such a large secret hidden?"

"None of your concern." Pandora said. "Do not interact with Fable. Heed my words."

Pandora snapped her fingers, within a blink of an eye she was gone. Denise lost for words once more. Shaking her head, rubbing her hand across her forehead.

IV

ONLY A CON COULD BREAK THIS STORY

Above Manchester, the clouds began to roar with thunder. Lightning flashed across the sky. Through the clouds, came down a man with the appearance of a general. Dressed in gold and red armor with a hint of white in the lining. He wore a golden helmet with only his glowing white eyes to be seen. He hovered in the air, looking down at the city.

"This is what they've managed to construct? This is what they perceive to be civilization! I have done much more and thus shall I do again."

He extended his arms and lightning poured out from the clouds onto the city. Striking the buildings and the streets. Cars drove off the roads to avoid the crashing bolts. The man laughed as he continued to maintain the bolts coming down. Elsewhere, the thunder could be heard, and Fable felt it from his home, going outside, he looked out, seeing the lightning bolts crashing.

"The hell is that?"

"That is Emblem." Pandora appeared from behind him. "And he has already begun his purpose."

"Then, why aren't you and the Four stopping him?" Fable wondered. "You have the power to do so."

"It is not our place."

"Not your place? But, it's mine?"

"This is your world. Your domain. You reside here. It is of your concern to deal with the Fallen King before he takes this world and merges it with the magical realm."

"I think you're all forgetting who I am. I'm a con artist who happens to know a lot about magic. I've lived in the magical realm for a time. Yes, I am human. This is my world. Yet, I am not the one who's set to take down some ancient dictator."

"But, you are. For I've seen your future. Standing side by side with others like yourself, taking on threats far greater than Emblem alone. This is only the beginning of your fate, Kurt Wesker. Do not throw it away out of the spirit of fear."

Fable sighed. Walking over to the table, he drank the remainder of the beer in the bottle and grabbed his duster from the wall. Putting it on, he approached the door before turning to Pandora.

"I'll see what I can do. But only on one condition?"

"Such is?"

"You stand beside me and face him."

"I can do that."

Fable nodded.

"Finally. Something she can do. Great."

Emblem continued to decimate Manchester as he glanced up

into the air, seeing a tear forming in between the realms. He yelled as the rift began to open. The physical world and the magic realm meeting. Inching closer together.

"I will create the perfect utopia. One many of which have yet to witness. A new world for all creatures. For all creation."

A quick blast came from the ground, hitting Emblem in the chest. As he felt the attack, the rift slowly closed. Emblem looked down toward the ground, where he saw Fable and Pandora. His eyes locked on Pandora.

"You live!"

"End this treachery, Emblem." Pandora commanded. "This is not the ancient time anymore."

"Still abiding by the rules! After all these eons, you have yet to learn the truth about independence."

"I know much. Though, I am not a traitor to my own kind or to my people!"

"Such folly coming from your mouth. Have you forgotten the lives you cost after the first failing?!"

"No. I have only learned to move on."

Fable glanced between the two. Confused and uneasy.

"What's going on here?" He asked.

Emblem came down to the streets. Standing before Fable and Pandora as the lightning bolts continued to fall.

"You managed to gain another apprentice." Emblem said.

"Apprentice? What does he mean?"

"This man is not my apprentice. He is here to stop you."

"A human? You've brought a human to stop me? Do you remember where we're from? The things we can do. The worlds we can shape and the lives we can destroy? We are gods among men, Pandora!"

"He's dissing me, isn't he?" Fable asked.

"Don't get distracted."

"I have an idea. Hold on."

Fable walked toward Emblem. No fear, though to be seen. Emblem stood still as Fable approached him. Pandora didn't make a move, only watched on. Fable stood up to Emblem, raising his head as Emblem's height far surpasses Fable's own.

"You're one tall dude."

"Have you come to kneel at my feet, human?"

"Kneel? No. I've come for a different reason."

"And what may that be?"

"Well, since this is our first encounter, I only have to ask one question."

"A question?"

"Do you like fireworks?"

"Fireworks?!"

"Yeah. Allow me to demonstrate."

Fable stepped back and from his side, he pulled out a smoke bomb. Tossing it into Emblem's face. Emblem fanned the smoke from his sight as Pandora rushed over, grabbing Emblem by his arms and slamming him into the pavement. Fable ran over and pulled out his revolver, loaded with magic-infused rounds. He aimed the gun toward Emblem's head.

"Over that fast?" Fable asked.

"Over?" Emblem said. "This is only the start of things to come!"

Emblem snapped his fingers and the storm ceased. A rift had opened as Emblem kicked Fable and Pandora from him. He jumped into the rift as it shut. Fable and Pandora looked around the spot, no sign of Emblem nor the rift.

"Aw man." Fable said. "I thought this would've gone much longer. I had him."

"No, you were toying with him."

"Trust me, I did more than just toy with the guy. Gave him something to remember me by."

"And what is that?"

"The smoke. wasn't exactly smoke. They were nano-sized fairies. Grabbed them from a pack of neo-witches. See, the fairies will place a tracking signal on Emblem wherever he goes, and the fairies are magic-resistance."

"That doesn't make any sense." Pandora said.

"I know. That's why it's not true."

"What?"

"Just highly-concentrated pixie dust I picked up from a card game."

Pandora shook her head in utter disgust with some shame, walking away from Fable.

"I will find Emblem. You have much to learn, Kurt Wesker."

"You're welcome. And Uh, it's Fable, Pandora. Fable. Remember. F. A. B. L.-"

"I know your name!"

Pandora disappeared from the area. Fable looked around, only to see some scared civilians and crashed vehicles. He nodded.

"Oh, well."

Fable went away and within the crowds of frightened people, Denise was there. Writing down everything she saw with every inch of detail possible.

I

<u>TREACHERY IN THE FAMILY</u>

A pair of well-armed men gather goods from a facility used by one of the top criminal organizations in London. Their faces covered with masks, dressed in black uniforms, wearing bulletproof vests, cargo pants, and boots. While packing up the boxes into the black van, three of them stand to the side, keeping watch of the area.

"Don't think any officers will come by tonight?"

"Nah. It's not the officers that concern me."

"Then who?"

"You heard about that figure that took out the guys at the warehouse some time ago?"

"Yeah. Thought it was just a made-up story."

"No. It happened. Guys in the group thought The Swordman came here to do some work. But, one of the men said it wasn't a man. But, a woman."

"Pfft! A woman?! I'm not falling for such a story."

"Why not? He told the officers it was a woman that took them all out. By herself."

"That's where I draw the line. No way a woman can take out that number of men on her own. Not possible. Science says so."

"That's the thing. There's something else about her. Something different."

"Only one thing different, she doesn't have balls. Simple math, boys."

Within the shadows, each of the men are taken out quickly and with sharp succession. Only leaving the three men speaking to one another. They turn, seeing the other men on the ground. Unconscious.

"What the hell?"

"What happened to them? I didn't even hear a thing."

"That's the whole purpose." said a voice from around them.

They turned around, scouting the area. Finding no one.

"Who said that?"

"I don't know, man. But, it's strange."

"Why is it strange?"

"Because it was a woman's voice."

One of the men turned back to the van, seeing something crouched atop the vehicle. He knew who it was. Aiming his gun.

"Shit! It's her!"

He began firing toward her as she dodged the rounds, moving from around the van to into the bushes nearby. The other two men looked around, not seeing what their ally has seen.

"She's here."

"That woman you spoke about?"

"Who else would I be talking about?"

"Nothing to worry yourself about. We'll take her out. End her little vigilante business quick, fast, and in a hurry."

They walked into the waist-high bushes of the field around them and quickly, she took out two of the men, leaving the one who did most of the disrespectful talk. He held his gun tightly, before it was grappled from him, falling into the bushes. He ran near the spot before being tripped. As he fell, he shook his head and rose up above the bushes, only to see the woman his ally spoke of.

"You have to be shitting me."

"Should've listened to your friend. He was telling the truth."

"You were the one who took out those guys at the warehouse? You?!"

"Who else did the man describe. From what I've heard, he said it was a woman. Don't I fit his description?"

"We don't need people like you in our country."

"Too bad. Besides, I'm from this country and I was born in this city. Technically, you're terrorizing my home."

"And what now? You've chose to stop it? Protect your city like those fools over in the West?"

"You could say that."

She kicked him in the face and he fell back into the bushes. Dazed.

"Remember to tell them my name when you wake up."

"Your name?"

"Yeah. You already know what it is."

She punched him as hard as she could. Knocking him out. Later, she searched the van, discovering the organizations involved in the operations. She shook her head reading the names listed on the file sheet.

"I'm closer to stopping you."

Folding the file sheet and placing it in her trench coat pocket, she left the area during the night. Leaving only the trail of unconscious thugs.

II

A NIGHT OUT

The next day, Cindy Lawson went walking with her close friend, Charlotte Queens. The two were out for a social call, grabbing a cup of coffee as they sat inside the coffee shop. Charlotte is mostly known for her red attire. Always dressed in either a red cloak or red scarf. A trademark of her own making. Her own dark hair matched even Cindy's. Cindy's apparel was one of a dark blue skirt and a black t-shirt. She also wore a scarf over her hair, reaching to the middle of her head.

"I have to ask. What happened with the case?"

"The case went well. Unfortunately, they didn't see things my way. But, it all worked out for the better."

"And what of your other duties?"

"What other duties?"

"Your sly ones during the night. Scouring around London like you're its Swordwoman."

"Funny."

"Speaking on that. Have you ever considered aiding those other heroes who have risen across the world?"

"I rather not. London is my territory."

"But, imagine the great things you can do. Like for example, you could travel to Manchester and aid their hero."

"The Fable guy? Not likely."

"He's nearby!"

"Not likely."

"Fine."

"What of your business?"

"Oh, I'm just cruising along. As always. Finding what fits me best."

In an office, Hale Prince, a fellow advocate for all Londoners prepared for his upcoming speech to the city. Most of the city has aligned themselves with Prince, while the others have agreed to the ideals of Cindy's Stepmother Anne. Prince and Anne have had disagreements for the past few months, leading them toward a political war to determine which one the city of London will side with.

During the fall of night, Cindy went out once more after gaining more information on her stepmother's plans for London. Leading her into the wilderness of Suffolk. While moving forward, she came across a strange odor. Covering her face from the stench. A rustling came from the bushes and quickly bolted out a shade, shoving Cinderella to the ground. Cindy looked, only seeing the shade's strange face and glowing red eyes.

"I've heard of you." Cinderella said.

Cinderella shoved the shade off her, standing up to face the strangeness. The shade morphed into a woman, wearing a dark cloak and ripped clothing. She carried a wooden staff with her.

"The Cannibalistic Witch." Cinderella uttered. "Never assumed you would be in Suffolk."

"I have a purpose to be here and I sensed your scent."

"Comforting. Why seek me out?"

"I have my orders."

"You're taking orders? From who?"

"None of your concern, Cinderella. All I have been assigned to do is to take you out. Kill you and your flesh shall be mine to consume."

"Not today."

Cinderella tossed a smoke bomb toward the Witch and tackled her to the ground. The Witch rose up and slammed the staff into the ground, causing a small tremor. Cinderella stood still as the Witch levitated and rushed toward her. Grabbing her by the throat. Cinderella began pounding the Witch's arm from her neck. Not knowing the full strength of the strange woman, Cinderella kicked the Witch in the face and stomped her into the ground.

"Who sent you?!" Cinderella yelled.

"Your theatrics will not work on me!"

"Maybe not. But, I know something will."

Cinderella pulled out a blade and sliced the Witch's arm. The Witch screeched with agony as the blade burned her skin. Cinderella held the blade over the Witch's head, set to strike.

"I know your weakness. Silver blade."

"I will never tell."

"Then, you leave me no choice."

Cinderella slammed her arm to kill the Witch, but she vanished into a portion of green mist. Cinderella searched the nearby areas and did not find her. Uncertain of the mystery, Cinderella continued her trail.

Hale Prince sat in his office reading a newspaper article titled 'The Cinderella Effect'. The article mentioned the existence of the rising heroes as well as Cinderella herself dwelling within London. Unsure of the article's facts, Hale set himself to discover the famed Cinderella after he has dealt with Stepmother Anne and her plans for the city.

Anne gathered her two daughters and arranged a plot to foil Prince's plans for the city. She sent out her daughters to meet with Hale secretly as they dressed in scandalous clothing, resembling such garments of a harlot. Anne's plan was simple. To have her daughters seduce Hale in the exchange of his downfall, giving her free reign to make the final decisions of London and Cinderella was closer to discovering the full truth.

III

<u>YOU HAVE A GIFT</u>

Hale continued to work in his office. A knock came from the door and he looked up, only to see Anne's daughters, Angelina and Alexis. They shut Hale's door and approached the desk.

"Excuse me, ladies, why are you in here?"

"We were told you were expecting us." Angelina said.

"Then, you were misinformed. I wasn't expecting anybody. Now, please leave my office as I have work to do."

"He doesn't want us in here, sister." Alexis uttered.

"I can see. We'll have to force it on him."

"You're not doing anything. Now, please leave my office."

"No wonder our mother will take over this place." Alexis said.

"Your mother?" Hale questioned.

"You know her. You call her Anne."

"She's your mother? And she sent you both here? To do what?"

"What do you think, genius?" Alexis giggled.

"Look at us and admit the truth. You wouldn't mind it."

"Your own mother sent her daughters to seduce her

competitor? Strange days indeed. But, there's nothing new under the sun."

"You would not deny us!" Alexis yelled.

"I just did. I am asking as politely as I can for the two of you to leave my office. Before I call security."

Alexis stormed out of the office with Angelina following. She gazed at Hale, rolling her eyes before slamming the office door. Hale chuckled as he sat back down to his desk.

"Strange days indeed."

Cinderella continued moving and found a place near Suffolk. The location was small, but unexpected by Londoners. She saw Anne speaking with a man. He was dressed in a trench coat and a fedora. She couldn't hear their conversation, but she saw a stack of boxes in the back of the man's van as he shut the door. He and Anne shook hands as he left the area.

"I will figure this out." Cinderella said to herself.

Cinderella made a return to her home and she sat down to meditate. During the meditation, she began to hear the voices of her father and mother. Her hands were held out and open. While the voices of her parents continued, a glow emitted from her hands as she began having visions of her past. Flashbacks with her parents to her training with the Creed of Swords. She opened her eyes, now glowing along with her hands. She balled her hands up in a fist and the glow decreased as did the glow in her eyes.

"You have a gift." Her mothers' voice echoed.

She stood up and checked the clock, seeing it's close to

midnight. She grabbed her coat and hat, leaving her home to confront her stepmother.

IV

<u>MIDNIGHT STRIKES</u>

Cinderella returned to the very same warehouse as before. When she arrived, she saw not only her stepmother present, but her daughters as well. Cinderella chuckled before making her entrance into the warehouse. As she opened the doors, she found herself surrounded by armed men. Anne turned around, seeing her. Angelina and Alexis were confused to Cindy's choice of apparel.

"Hold on." Anne said. "Cindy?"

"Anne."

"What are you doing here and why are you dressed like that?"

"I have my reasons. I know what you're planning."

"Wait. The guys that were attacked in this place sometime ago, that was your doing?"

"Who else?" Cinderella smirked. "I'm doing what others refuse to do."

"Cindy is the Cinderella?" Angelina asked.

"Not possible." Alexis said. "She's too soft to do such a thing."

"I'm more than you realize. This city has suffered enough harm from people like you. I've come to bring a balance."

"You're treading on some dangerous waters, girl."

"Danger helps the cause."

Anne stepped forward, approaching Cindy. The two stood face to face. Anne was several inches taller than Cindy. Anne smirked.

"Don't follow this path. Being a hero. It won't end well for someone like you. You know better than this."

"True. But, I also know right from wrong and what you're plotting is beyond such natural evil."

"Hmm." Anne uttered.

She glanced at her watch, stepping back from Cindy. She signaled the armed men to approach Cinderella as she and the daughters prepared themselves.

"This isn't over." Cinderella said.

"I know. This should give you a fresh start."

The daughters left the warehouse. Anne looked back at Cindy and shook her head.

"I'm going to miss you very much."

"Touching."

"Midnight strikes, Cinderella."

Anne signaled the men to attack Cinderella and they rushed her. She attacked their legs and arms. Elbowing a few in their neck. She looked up and tossed a shuriken, breaking the light bulbs. Placing the warehouse into darkness. There, she began using stealth attacks to knock out the guards one by one. Cinderella exited the warehouse, only to see Anne and the daughters leaving in a car. Cindy could only stare and she watched closely.

While returning home, Cinderella was confronted by a strange force. Unseen by the natural eye as it grabbed her and tossed her into a nearby wall. She stood up, looking around. There was nothing. She returned to her home to receive a phone call. A call from Travis Vail, the Spirit-Seeker. Something urgent has happened and it requires the Sly Detective's skill set.

HEAVEN HAS CALLED:
ALL CALLED FROM ABOVE

I

AFTERLIFE VISITOR

Gabriel Abraham turned around in his office, staring at the door. Where Travis Vail, the Spirit-Seeker stood. Vail had his hands in his coat pocket with a stern look on his face. Abraham was confused to Vail's unknown and sudden visit.

"Too soon." Vail said grinning.

"Why are you here?"

"Something's happening, and I can't handle it on my own."

"What do you mean?"

"Something huge. There's a powerful force that's rising beneath the earth. Preparing to make an entrance into our world. One that will certainly end all on this world."

"Demonic force?"

"Stronger."

"Good to see you two here." A voice said, coming from the lobby area of Abraham's Revelation Center.

Vail and Abraham left the office to find the stranger, standing in the lobby. He was of African descent and was dressed modestly. Brown slacks, shoes, with a long-sleeve shirt and vest. He also wore a black fedora. Vail and Abraham have never seen the man before in the fields.

"Who are you?" Vail asked.

"How did you get in?" Abraham questioned.

"Front door was open. Figured I would make myself in and on serious purpose."

"Your name, lad?" Vail said.

"Name stays with me. But, those in our field of work call me Papa Afterlife."

"Papa Afterlife?" Abraham said. "What kind of name is that?"

"Afterlife? As in the magician Papa Afterlife?"

"That would be me."

"Hmm." Vail said. "Funny, you're different that I thought."

"You know this man?"

"No. but, I've heard of his work across the Atlantic. Done some things in Africa, India, places as such."

"Good. Then, you have an idea as to why I'm here."

"Something of the sort."

"Now, what is this thing of serious purpose?"

"There's a dark force coming. Almost near the physical plane of this existence. I was planning on paying you both a visit at your residence. But, given the tow of you here now, makes the message all easier."

"And the message is?"

"This force is ancient. Very ancient. You came across the sin entity during your mission overseas, Vail. You've already sensed the power. Plus, there's a stronger entity roaming around called the Sin Phantom. The Phantom was already chased down by the Death Chaser and is still on the loose."

"Death Chaser?" Abraham said. "There's no such thing as one of them."

"You haven't been studying much have you." Afterlife uttered. "The Death Chaser has been around for ages. You'll need his help in stopping this coming threat."

"You're here to tell us to form a team?" Vail smirked. "Like the heroes over after the Retropolis incident."

"Something along those lines. Because, this threat cannot be stopped with just the two of you. You'll need a unit. One made up of detectives like yourselves, and other forces at work. Spiritual assassins, cryptids, anything you can get to muster up enough power to send this force back into the prison where it belongs."

"And will you be a part of this team?" Abraham asked.

"I'll be watching. An overseer if you so ask."

"Great." Vail said. "Watching from the sidelines."

"I can do more when I'm invisible to the enemy. Soon, you may find that out."

"One can only dream, sunshine."

Afterlife turned away, approaching the door. He stopped, turning back toward Vail and Abraham.

"Unify your members. You do not have much time."

Afterlife exited the Center. Vail turned to Abraham, who was confused about the entire scenario.

"You think Cinderella will be of use to us?"

"We'll have to ask her." Vail said. "Right now, we need to

gather some information on possible recruits. If what Afterlife is saying is true, we will need all the help we can get."

II

CALLING THOSE THAT ARE ABOVE

Vail and Abraham set out on their journey to recruit the members possible for their unit. After doing some digging, Vail came up with a list of names. Through much research and sightings across the world, the names he chose were the ones felt closest to the possible unit.

"Where are we headed first?" Abraham asked.

"Chicago. There's a man out there who calls himself the Spiritual Assassin. Figured giving him a look will determine much more."

"His name?"

"John Terror." Vail said. "Supposedly, he's a nubreed."

"One of them. I see."

"Plus, he was in Retropolis during their incident. Means he's in good company with the rising heroes. Maybe he knows more than we do."

Vail and Abraham traveled from D.C. to Chicago. There, they came across a place in the outskirts of the city. Away from the public. They looked around, it's quiet and still.

"He's here?" Abraham asked.

"Said to be. Might as well knock on the door."

Abraham knocked, the door opened. They didn't see Terror, but they saw his ally.

"Who are you guys?"

"We're detectives." Vail said. "Looking for John Terror. Heard he resides at this place."

"And how would you know that?"

"Like I said, lad, we're detectives."

"Then, you're pretty sloppy." A voice said from behind Vail and Abraham.

"Shit." Abraham said.

They turned around to see terror himself standing behind them with two guns pointed at their heads. Vail smirked while Abraham was unsure of what to do. Terror looked at the young man standing at the door.

"Carl, go inside. You two, follow him."

"Sure thing." Vail said.

They followed Carl into the hideout of Terror. They were placed at the chairs near the working table. Terror approached them, removing his black trench coat and sunglasses. He sat in front of them, measuring them from their size to potential skill set.

"I know what you're doing." Vail uttered.

"Good." Terror replied. "Now, tell me, why are two strange detectives suddenly at my door?"

"We're not ordinary detectives." Abraham said. "We're occult detectives."

"Occult detectives?"

"Yes." Vail said. "He is Gabriel Abraham. Known as the Devilhunter of Washington D.C. You've heard of the Revelation Center, haven't you?"

"Once or twice. And you are?"

"Travis Vail, the Spirit-Seeker. I travel much."

"Ok, so why are you here? Why come to me? And what for?"

"We are recruiting possible members for a team. There's a supernatural threat coming, and it could very well-"

"Not this shit again."

"What?" Vail asked. "What shit?"

"I've done my team shares with those heroes."

"The Retropolis Incident? We know all about it. That tells us, you aligned yourself with those major heroes. Swordman and the like. I have to ask, was this before or after The Swordman confronted the Mutant-thing in the woods?"

"How should I know?"

"Then, how did the two of you meet?"

"We had some similar business. Taking down the same crime lords. We had an early scuffle, but, we're on good terms now."

"Splendid to hear. Then, you don't mind joining yourself with us."

"I'm not a team player. I did what I had to do in Retropolis for those who couldn't defend themselves."

"I get that." Vail said. "But, I have to ask, if the opportunity arose once more, would you take it?"

"Instead of just a city, it's the world." Abraham said. "Much larger than what you're accustomed to."

"How large of a threat are we talking?"

"One that could wipe out all life on this earth and perhaps breach the spiritual planes."

"That bad, huh?"

"It is." Abraham said. "So, what do you say?"

Terror nodded.

"When the time comes, I'll be there."

"How can we be sure of that?" Abraham asked.

"Lend some trust my way. You'll see I'm telling the truth."

"Fair enough." Vail said. "May we leave now?"

"By all means."

Vail and Abraham left Terror's hideout. Returning to Vail's vehicle. They sat inside as Vail looked over the other names. Vail circled Terror's name.

"Who's next?" Abraham asked.

"A friend in London. Figured she would help us out."

"Off to London. Again."

Traveling to London, they waited near the Big Ben once again at night. Abraham looked around for her as he did before.

"She's not here yet?"

"I gave her a phone call." Vail said. "She knows we're here."

Sliding down the walls of Big Ben was Cinderella. She landed, standing in front of the two occult detectives. They hugged each other with smiles. A rare thing to see in their fields.

"I got the call." Cinderella said. "What is it this time?"

"We need your help. Again. Only this time, it involves a more powerful force."

"How powerful?"

"Strong enough to wipe out all life and enter the spiritual dimensions."

"Well, this all sounds like a lot to handle. I'm still in an ongoing investigation."

"If this force rises, you won't have any investigations to cover. Cindy, please, you have to align with us and take out."

"That bad?" Cinderella asked.

"It is."

"Confronting the Mutant-Thing was fun. I guess I can add in the spare time."

"Great." Vail said. "Now, we wait."

"For what?" Abraham asked.

"Cindy wasn't the only one I contacted."

"Who else is in London besides me?"

"An old soul."

From the ground erupted a white mist. Surrounding Vail, Abraham, and Cinderella. The mist turned, morphing into itself, forming an astral body. The body formed and stood before them. Wearing clothing from the Victorian era. The body was of a man. Vail applauded the entrance.

"Abraham, Cindy, meet Robert Shaw. Or as the folktales call him, the Ghost of England."

"The Ghost of England?" Cinderella said. "I thought that was only a story."

"It's more than a story, lass. See, you're looking at him."

"Travis Vail, Spirit-Seeker." Shaw said. "Gabriel Abraham, the Devilhunter. Cindy Lawson, known as Cinderella. I stand before the three of you this night to declare my allegiance to your cause."

"That was easy." Abraham said.

"I figured you may know this we don't." Vail said. "Is there anything we don't know?"

"Best for you to meet with the Unholy Knight called Creed and the Death Chaser, a Soul of Retribution."

"Creed and the Death Chaser?" Cinderella asked.

"Me and Abraham were already told about meeting the Chaser. Trust me, that is soon to come. But, about this Creed fellow, where can we find him?"

"I will guide you to him. But, beware of his aggression. For he is keen to discovering the rising force that threats this world."

"Duly noted." Vail said. "Then, let's get going."

III

THE UNHOLY KNIGHT
AND
THE SOUL OF RETRIBUTION

Returning to the States, Vail, Abraham, and Cinderella are guided by the Ghost of England toward an old church in the Northwest counties. Reaching near the city of Hartford, Connecticut. The Ghost of England signaled a peculiar church building. One with a large black cross standing atop the structure.

"I've been there before." Vail said.

"What for?" Cinderella asked.

"Exorcism of a old man. However, Connecticut is filled with much paranormal and demoric activity. I know from experience."

"And is this where we find this Creed?" Abraham asked Shaw.

"Yes. He will be here soon. Trust my words."

"How soon?" Vail uttered. "I'm just curious is all."

"Soon."

"Tonight? Tomorrow morning? Next week? When? You must

have a particular clue."

"You'll see."

"I guess I will."

The Ghost turned to face the group and his eyes shined upon the cross. Yet, he caught movement atop the structure. Vail caught his glimpse and gazed up himself.

"What is it, Trav?" Cinderella asked.

"We've found him. Or, he's found us."

The moving object lunged down toward them, landing on its feet in front of them. They stepped back as the dark blue cloak edged itself back to reveal Creed himself. Creed raised up from his bent position of the landing. Standing tall, facing the unit. His golden eyes gazed at them. His cloak echoing the sound of a chilling wind.

"Who are you?" Creed asked.

"We're detectives." Vail said. "Besides the Ghost here."

"We have no intention of bothering you." Abraham declared. "But, we need your assistance with a dire cause."

"The world is full of causes. Mine aren't sealed in the natural realm."

"Which is why we're here." Vail said. "There's a powerful force rising from beneath the earth. If we don't stop it soon, it will wipe out all life. Everything. Humans. Animals. Plant life. All of it."

"Where is the origin of this threat?"

"I... I don't know."

"Then you are wasting your time."

"Please, listen to us." Vail said, grabbing a hold of Creed's arm.

"Best you remove your hand before you have it no longer."

Vail pulled back his hand from Creed. Smirking.

"You must have some knowledge of a powerful force. Something."

"You speak not of the cryptic Zone."

"Don't think so. I thought that place was sealed."

"It is sealed." Creed said. "I and a fellow angel closed its portals from opening across the world."

"Then, it can't be someone from the Cryptic Zone." Abraham said. "Vail, what do you think it could be?"

"I'm working on it."

From behind them, a spiraling flame emitted from thin air. Causing them to turn around, startling them without haste. Creed stood in front of them, his cloak flowing roughly, his claws sharpened and his gaze keen.

"The hell is that?" Cinderella asked.

"I've seen such a thing before." Vail said.

"Where?" Abraham wondered.

"It's the entrance of the Death Chaser."

The Death Chaser walked out of the spiraling flame and shut its door behind him. He stood face to face with Creed. Two opposing forces of the supernatural realm.

"The Unholy Knight." The Death Chaser said.

"A Soul of Retribution." Creed remarked.

"What's going on here?" Vail asked.

"I should ask you the same, Travis Vail." The Death Chaser said. "I have been tracking all your movements since you were visited by Papa Afterlife."

"Seriously?" Abraham asked.

"Don't feel too bad. It's his job."

"Death Chaser." The Ghost of England said. "Tell us of your purpose here. What do you know of this rising power?"

"More than all of you combined."

"That's good to know." Vail uttered.

"The rising force is a malevolent entity known as Demonticronto. My sworn adversary. Me and my liege were dealing with a soldier of his. A sin phantom."

"Sin Phantom?" Abraham asked. "The hell."

"Don't be too shocked. I know what he's speaking of. I came across this sin phantom during my investigation in Italy. It's a powerful foe. But, a lieutenant demon protected me from its wrath."

"What demon?" The Death Chaser asked.

"Kamagrauto. Heard of him?"

"I have."

"Who is Kamagrauto?" Abraham asked with confusion. "What is going on here?"

"We can explain later, Abraham. For right now, we need to focus on how to stop this Demonticronto demon from rising."

"Creed, Death Chaser." Shaw said. "Align yourselves this day with them. Aid them in stopping Demonticronto and the Sin Phantom."

"I will aid you." Death Chaser said. "Only to stop Demonticronto from causing much harm to this reality."

"As will I." Creed said.

"Excellent." Vail said. "Now, all we need is some guidance on finding a place where Demonticronto's power is growing."

A great flash of white light pierced through he air. Causing a rift between realms. Everyone covered their eyes from the great shine except for Creed and Death Chaser, who are immune to such power. From the rift appeared a man dressed in black with an midnight blue cloak, white gloves and a hat. His long white hair stood out amongst his white facial hair and shining eyes. His pupils could not be seen.

"Who are you supposed to be?" Vail asked.

"I am the Visitant Outlander and I have come to guide you all in this quest you have taken upon yourselves.

IV

THE BROTHERLESS ONE
AND
THE WRATH OF YAH

"Visitant Outlander?" Vail asked. "My, I thought you were just a myth. Hidden away by the ancestors of old."

"I am very real as I stand here before your very eyes."

"I can see that. Which means the other guy exists as well."

"He does."

Vail nodded.

"This is great."

"I don't get what's happening here?" Cinderella asked. "Why have you come to help us? We have Creed and the Death Chaser for that."

"All of you combined together cannot stop Demonticronto's grown power and with the Sin Phantom at his side. I have come to grant an offering to you."

"What kind of offering, lad?"

"To lock away Demonticronto."

"Lock him up?" Abraham asked. "What on earth for?"

"There is no prison that can keep the sin fire from burning Demonticronto." The Death Chaser said. "I will kill him when it comes."

"You shouldn't" Outlander said. "For Demonticronto's existence serves a much greater cause."

"I thought the greater cause was to take him out." Vail said. "Eliminate the evil. Put away the evil. Not imprison it so it can break out."

"Killing such a powerful force will only cause more tragedy than peace."

"And how would you be aware of such causes?" Creed asked "What happened in the past to alter someone's mind such as yours of a simple cause?"

"I've been around for ages. Much longer than this physical realm. I know what happens when the greater plan is thwarted or tapped."

"Now, I get it." Vail uttered.

"Get what?" Cinderella asked.

"Why the other guy doesn't like Outlander here. He's too into the whole justice motif."

"What other guy?" Abraham wondered.

"He's here." Vail grinned, looking up.

Like a falling cloud, he came down from the night sky. Cloaked in a dark violet cloak and hood. Only his red eyes were visible unto the shining of his presence caused his face to appear. Brighter than Outlander's light. His amulet glowed like the sun.

he approached Outlander, standing toe to toe with him.

"Dark Manhunter." Outlander said. "The walking embodiment of the Wrath of Yah."

"Visitant Outlander." Manhunter said. "The Brotherless One. Looking for a way to assist all humanity in its endeavors."

"This is good to hear." Vail said. "Now, we don't need a scuffle between two cosmic forces. Not yet anyway. Manhunter, may I get your view on all of this?"

"Demonticronto must be killed. Execute him before more damage is done."

"Killing him will only bring more harm into this world." Outlander said. "You're speaking tragedy upon their lives."

"Their lives will only find peace when those like Demonticronto and the Sin Phantom are eliminated from existence. Permanently."

"Then, it's settled." Vail said. "We take down Demonticronto."

"As we should." Chaser said. "I will give the final blow."

"Oh, will you and Outlander be joining us on this journey?"

"We will be around." Manhunter said. "Right on time."

"I'll take your word for it."

Manhunter and Outlander vanished from their sight. Vail looked around, seeing everyone else still standing by. He nodded. Impressed.

"Now, all we need is one more member."

"And who is that going to be?" Cinderella wondered.

"A fellow friend from Retropolis."

"Come on." Cinderella said. "He's not going to stop what he's doing just to help us out.”

“I’m not talking about him. I’m speaking of the other guy.”

Cinderella thought for the moment. Abraham signed and Vail grinned.

“Oh. Him.”

V

THE MUTANT-THING RISES

The unit traveled to the city of Retropolis. Upon arriving, they noticed the city was under a minor form of martial law. Streets were still and quiet. There was hardly anybody along the sidewalks or outside.

"What's been happening here?" Vail wondered.

"I guess he's cleaning the city faster than I would expect." Cinderella said.

"Hmm." Vail replied.

"Whatever happened to John Terror joining us?" Abraham asked.

"Funny you mention that. I called him as we were headed this direction. He said he would meet us in the wilderness."

"Meet us there? Why not here?"

"Out in the open I guess."

"We must reach this forest soon." Shaw said. "I can sense Demonticronto's power surging from below our feet."

"Understood." Vail said.

Entering the dark forest near Retropolis, they traced their steps from before, coming across a large crater-sized hole in the ground.

"This was the spot." Abraham said.

"I remember." Vail replied.

"How do you plan to conjure him?" Cinderella asked.

In the distance, motorcycle sounds entered the forest. They turn back, seeing Terror getting off his bike, walking toward their direction. Vail waved his hands for Terror to see.

"Good thing he's here." Abraham said.

"We'll see for sure."

"I told you I would come on my time."

"Yeah. Right after I called you."

"Seemed like the right moment." Terror grinned. "Now, why are you all out here in the woods? At night?"

"Here to find an old friend." Vail said.

"I wouldn't call him a friend." Abraham gestured.

"Then what is he?"

"A monster." Cinderella said. "One of cryptid origins."

"Nice to know."

Death Chaser started to move around the area. His eyes gazed on the surroundings. As he turned, facing the city. He pointed with great intension. The unit wasn't sure to what he was seeing.

"The Phantom." Chaser said. "He's in the city."

"Are you sure?" Vail asked.

"I know."

"Well, I have an idea." Cinderella said. "Why don't we split up."

"How so?" Abraham questioned.

"Me, Shaw, and the Chaser go find this Sin Phantom while you, Vail, Terror, and Creed summon up the big creature."

"I'm not for this, Cindy." Vail said. "But, since what Chaser said is true, best be going, lass."

Cinderella nodded as she, Shaw, and the Chaser went back into Retropolis. Vail sighed, turning back to the crater in the ground. He stepped into it. Stomping the soil, twisting his foot.

"What are you doing?" Terror asked.

"Waking the big fellow up."

"And he's just going to pop up out of that hole?"

"I hope so. Otherwise, I'm dirtying up my shoes." Vail smirked.

Cinderella, Shaw, and the Chaser walked on he road within Retropolis. Still no one outside. The Chaser moved faster than the two, walking near an alleyway. Cinderella and Shaw followed him. Discovering him coming to a stop, where they saw the Sin Phantom himself.

"You've found me." The Phantom said.

"I'm sending you away." The Chaser said.

"You're not supposed to be here." Cinderella gestured.

"Then, where can I go?"

"To the pit!" Chaser yelled.

Chaser emitted sin fire from his hands and threw it at the Phantom, who dodged the flames. Cinderella ran toward him, trying to grab him by his throat. The Phantom morphed his body into a transparent form, causing Cinderella to slip as he snatched her by the coat and tossed her against the Chaser. Shaw levitated toward the Phantom. Both entities staring down.

"You have violated the natural law." Shaw said.

"And you are going to lecture me on law? I know your history. Robert Shaw. Don't assume yourself as one of the helpless."

"My past is dead. Just as your soul!"

Shaw went to touch the Phantom, but the Phantom grabbed him by his head and his hand glowed like a blue flame above Shaw. He shook himself, trying to get free and as he reached for the Phantom's arm, he was let go.

"Shaw?" Cinderella yelled.

"He's currently occupied right now." Phantom said. "You will have to wake him up."

Shaw's ghostly body arose from the ground, facing Cinderella and the Chaser. The Chaser stepped forward, sensing something odd with Shaw.

"Stand behind me, Cinderella."

"What's wrong?"

"The Phantom, he's done something to Shaw."

"Like mind control?"

"No. he's awoken the once living nature when his being. Sin has crawled back into his soul. Wickedness is consuming him."

"What can we do?"

"We can beat it out of him. He's only a spirit. Not living flesh."

"Do well with such." The Phantom said. "I must be going. See you all soon when my master arrives!"

The Phantom vanished. Shaw's sin-filled spirit rushed toward the Chaser, grabbing him by the throat and holding him close.

Cinderella attended to punch Shaw, but him as a spirit, she was powerless.

"Poor girl." Shaw said. "You're no help once more."

"You leave the woman out of this." The Chaser said. "I will cleanse your spirit of the sin that has entered you!"

"Why? I've never felt more alive."

"You're not alive. You're dead."

Vail, Abraham, Terror, and Creed stood around the crater. Vail reached into his pocket, pulling out his ritual book. Terror was confused, standing amongst a group of men he's never met. He gazed toward Creed, looking at his flowing cloak.

"How does that work?"

"It works with my mind." Creed said.

"Is that so." Terror replied. "I guess it works wonders."

"When it needs be."

"I'm going to read this ritual in Latin." Vail said. "It should summon the big fellow."

"Why Latin?" Terror questioned.

"It works for circumstances like this."

"What of Hebrew, Greek, Arabic, or Persian?"

"I've dabbled in it before. Best be careful with those if you ask me."

Terror nodded. "I see."

"Are you sure this will work properly?" Abraham asked.

"You were with us last time, remember?"

"This isn't like last time. He knows who we are."

"He doesn't know Creed or Johnny boy. We'll be fine."

Abraham shook his head and Vail grinned. Opening the book,

turning the pages. He stopped and looked at the three around him.

"Ready?"

"Sure." Abraham said.

"Proceed." Creed said.

"Go for it." Terror gestured. "I'm curious."

Vail stood steady, gazing into the crater. His eyes focused on the page within the book. One hand stretched outward over the crater.

"*Voco super te, qui habitas in terra ejus qui creavit elementa. Ergo surge, et sta in conspectu nostro.*"

The crater began to glow a bright green. They stepped back as the dirt flew into the air, falling upon them like heavy rain. After the dirt had fell and settled, their eyes were focused on who was standing in the middle of the crater. Vail smiled.

"You rose!"

Vail approached the Mutant-Thing. Standing in the center of the crater. His appearance hadn't' changed since their last encounter. Mutant-Thing looked around, seeing Abraham, Terror, and Creed. He looked down toward Vail.

"Travis Vail." The Mutant-Thing said.

"Listen, bog fellow. We're here on important notice. Not like last time."

"Why have you truly come? Why disturb my slumber?"

"Because there's a powerful force preparing to rise from beneath the earth. If it does, it has the potential to destroy everything."

"What is the destroyer's name?"

"Demonticronto apparently."

"Hmm." Mutant-Thing uttered. "His power is great. He was defeated ages ago by those such as yourselves. But, I see you're missing several warriors"

"They're currently busy finding a sin phantom. Working for Demonticronto it seems."

"And you require my aid in taking Demonticronto down?"

"Yes." Vail said. "That is why we're truly here. Honestly."

Mutant-Thing turned, seeing Creed. He pointed toward him, letting the others look and see.

"He is unholy. Made of malevolent origins. How can he be trusted in such a time?"

"I rebelled against the one who formed me in such manner."

"I smell the stench of the Cryptic Zone on you."

"I was chosen as an apprentice to Adrambadon, Lord of the Cryptic Zone. His demands were dire. But, over time, I broke from his grasp and chosen to make a better change with this curse he has bestowed upon me."

"No matter. He has power over you as long as you're connected to the source."

"Not to cut off this contact." Vail said. "But, we're going to need Creed in order to stop Demonticronto and his little sin lad roaming on about."

"As you say. I will give my aid to this cause. Only to help the earth remain in its current stead."

"Understood." Vail said. "How will this work now? When we find the phantom and Demonticronto, how will you help us? Am I to summon you once more?"

"When the time comes, you will know of my help."

"That's it?" Vail questioned. "A tight, but small riddle."

"Take it for what it's worth, Spirit-Seeker. Now, leave this forest. I must return to my slumber."

"Fair enough."

The Mutant-Thing burrowed himself into the crater as the dirt covered him completely.

"Now what?" Terror asked.

"We find the others. Tell them it's time we come up with a plan."

"Hopefully, they've captured the Sin Phantom first." Abraham said. "Save us all some time."

"Let's find out."

The Chaser and Shaw fought one another with Cinderella giving slight aid to the Chaser. A ring of sinfire had surrounded the sin-corrupted Shaw. Cinderella moved over, standing next to the Chaser.

"You must be purged once more." The Chaser commanded.

"You can't take away such a feeling. I can feel pleasure again. Lust. Greed. I can sense them all."

"That is why I must do this. Only for the purity of your soul."

The Chaser balled up his fist and quickly, the sin fire had rose from the ground, consuming Shaw. The others arrived as they saw Shaw within the flames and chaser with Cinderella standing back.

"The hell's going on?!" Vail yelled.

"The Sin Phantom planted a seed within Shaw's mind. He

became consumed with sin. I am purging it from his spirit form."

"Is he still in there?" Abraham asked.

"Yes." Cinderella said. "Chaser is burning the sin seed out of him."

Shaw continued to burn, and the Chaser opened his hand, ceasing the spiral sin fire as it returned to the ground, only leaving Shaw's spirit remaining. They ran over toward him. Chaser placed his hand upon Shaw's head.

"How is he?" Cinderella asked.

"He's still in there. The sin is gone."

"Just like that, you burned it out of him?" Terror asked.

"Yes. This is my line of work."

"Would be nice to have all humans enter this treatment."

"It would kill them." The Chaser said. "They're still in their mortal forms. The human body cannot handle such pain from sinfire."

Shaw's eyes opened as he arose from the ground, looking at his body.

"You purged it from me."

"As I only could."

"Now, since that's out of the way, we need to make a plan and quickly." Vail said. "I fear Demonticronto's is not as far away as we assume."

"He isn't." The Chaser said.

"And how are you aware of his whereabouts?" Abraham asked.

"I can sense him. He's walking upon the earth right now and he isn't far from our location."

"Then, you can track him."

"I can."

"Then, let's get going." Vail uttered.

VI

THEY HAVE BEEN CALLED

The unit followed the Chaser out of Retropolis and have stumbled upon a cemetery near the United States border. The cemetery was calm, quiet, and still. Vail shrugged his shoulders walking past the headstones on the ground.

"What is it now?" Cinderella asked Chaser.

"He's here." Chaser said. "He is here."

"Where?" Vail wondered. "Is he under the ground or standing in front of us? Just invisible?"

Dirt kicked up from a grave as the Sin Phantom made himself known once more. The unit stood their ground toward the Phantom, who did not move past the gravesite.

"You've come." The Phantom said.

"No shit, lad." Vail replied. "You know why we're here."

"I do, and he is proud to have you here. To bear witness to his uprising."

"Then, where is the bastard?"

"Where's Demonti?!" The Chaser yelled.

"He's right here."

He grave turned into molten lava within seconds and created an opening in the ground, a deep pit. The Phantom moved from the grave as lava flew up in the air, yet, not falling back toward the ground.

"You see what I'm seeing?" Vail asked Cinderella.

"Yeah. I do."

Within the lava, the unit could see something moving. Hovering within the lava. As the lava settled its pouring, the figure could be seen. His red-skin, torn tunic, and long fiery hair. He landed on his feet beside the Phantom.

"There you are!" The Chaser said.

"Yes. I am here."

"Demonticronto I presume." Abraham gestured.

"In the flesh as they say."

"You've come to the wrong place, fellow."

"Oh, have I?"

"We're sending you back into your prison." Abraham said.

"I give you the opportunity to try."

The Chaser grunted, running toward Demonticronto with his arms covered in sin fire. The Chaser went for an attack but speared to the ground by the Phantom with a quickening force.

"You and I have a score to settle, Retributor."

"You've forgotten me." Shaw said, tackling the Phantom.

The unit began their battle with Demonticronto. Creed went for the aerial attack as Demonti's height was near thirteen feet tall. Demonti's strength from his arms, knocked Creed from the air, as well as his dragon-like tail, swiping Vail, Abraham, and Cinderella off their feet.

"This is depressionaly easy." Demonti grinned.

"*'Depressionaly*?" Cinderella said. "Is that a word?"

"Doesn't matter." Vail said. "We're not here to learn new words."

Vail chanted out a binding spell, causing the air around Demonti to constrict him. Holding him steady while Creed attacked him from his head to his torso. Abraham also chanted a spell to keep Demonticronto still. Meanwhile, the Chaser and Sin Phantom battled it out through the cemetery. Chaser snatched Phantom by his neck and tossed him against a headstone. Phantom dodged an incoming punch from Chaser with sinfire dripping from his fist. Shaw went for an attack of his own yet tripped by the Phantom.

"This is sad for your kind." Demonticronto said. "I assumed humanity had learned the means of working with such magic feats."

Demonti increased his strength, breaking the spiritual bonds around him, knocking down Vail, Cinderella, and Abraham. He grabbed Creed's cloak and slammed him into the ground. Terror ran up, firing shots with his pistols. Demonti grabbed the pistols, slapping Terror with them and stomping on his back. Demonticronto savored the moment.

"You're no match for me. I am above such primitive feats."

"I've heard that before." Cinderella said.

"Haven't we all."

The sky quickly opened above the cemetery and from there, Visitant Outlander and Dark Manhunter appeared before them.

Standing in front of Demonticronto. He moved from the downed team and stepped forward to Outlander and Manhunter.

"The two of you, working as one? Impressive."

"Don't take this lightly, demon." Manhunter said.

"You have trespassed upon a realm you have no authority."

"Spare the reasoning, Eidolon. I have come for my purpose only."

"And your purpose shall be?"

"To rule over Man. As the others should have done eons ago."

"That is where you're wrong." Manhunter said, raising his hand.

"You cannot end me." Demonti said. "I am still needed. I know the end of all this. I am not a fool."

"Yet, you know the end and continue to act as such." Outlander said. "No, we will send you back to your realm until the opportune time arises according to the Word. However, this team of outcasts have revealed they're just as a match for you when the time comes."

"Look at them! They're not a match for me!"

"So, you truly do not know the end of all things." Manhunter said. "Go home, demon."

Manhunter conjured up a portal beneath Demonti's feet and he fell into the deep lighted pit. The Phantom also was pulled from the Chaser's grasp and dragged into the pit. Once they were inside, the pit closed at the command of Manhunter. Then, the area was still once more. The unit returned to their feet, approaching the embodiments of justice and vengeance.

"I'm confused." Vail said. "What's happened here?"

"Demonti knows of his end." Outlander said. "This day was not such."

"The end?" The Chaser uttered. "I know his end for I have seen it."

"You have, Soul of Retribution." Manhunter said. "But, this is not the day."

"Hold on." Vail said. "When is this end you're speaking of?"

"Soon." Outlander said. "Sooner than the world will know. For the end is near and it is right at the door."

"As in the days of Noah and such like?"

"You know the details, Spirit-Seeker." Manhunter said. "For a dark force will return to this world and claim it as his own. Many will fall at his feet in opposition and will rise once more. For now, continue as such and you will succeed."

"Fair enough."

"Best you all go your own ways." Outlander said. "Demonti will not return quickly as you will imagine. For there are other threats that pose damage to this world and the realms. When the time comes, you all will be united once more. For you all are *Heaven's Called.*"

"Yet, you will not know the day, the time, nor the hour." Manhunter said. "We bid your farewell. For now."

Outlander and Manhunter disappeared from their sights. Vail looked back at everyone and chuckled.

"Well, shit."

Afterwards, they each returned to their domains. Creed and

Death Chaser continued their spiritual work, Cinderella and Shaw returned to London, Abraham made it back to the Revelation Center in D.C. and Vail continued his work across the world. Yet somewhere secretly, a stash of grimoires had been taken by an unknown group. A group led by a priest who has a past with Vail.

DOCTOR DARK: HOLDER OF DARKNESS

I

THE WANDERING IMMORTAL

A plethora of murders have been committed across the earth grounds. The victims vary between men, women, children, animals, and the environment. The murders were detailed to have begun months prior, although many ignored the early signs that came before it. It was not until sometime later when the humans began to cry out for help concerning the murders. Many are now parentless, brotherless, sisterless, husbandless, wifeless, childless, petless, homeless, and now they call for help. They want the help and they want it now.

"So, I will go into the searching to find out what has taken their possessions and why. A matter such as this cannot go unchecked or underhanded."

Darkous, the Keeper of the Cosmos, also known as Doctor Dark and Randolph Dark to humanity, travels through the earth to every location where a murder has been committed. From various street alleys to city parks to construction sites to day cares to neighborhood homes to animal shelters. While searching, Darkous looked at humanity and what they are doing at the sites. Most simply are minding their own business, particularly have forgotten about the murders and are now busy with the cares of this world and obsessed with celebrities and self-indulgence.

While looking into a museum that was closed down due to a murder, Darkous found a unusual fabric on the wooden floor. The fabric was covered in the colors of dark violet and gold. It shined throughout anything else on the floor and inside the museum. He picked it up and analyzed it from the other fabrics throughout the history of Man. Darkous sniffed the fabric, sensing it to be soaked in magic.

"It must be him again. I can feel his aura."

Darkous took the fabric and evaporated from the museum and into the Astral Dimension realm. He travels through the dimension, through its various color changes from violet to green to blue to white and repeating itself. Walking through, Darkous comes across Beatrice, one of the Astral Entities, such is Darkous. Beatrice greeted Darkous as he walked through the dimension.

"A pleasure to gaze upon you once more, Darkous."

"I am here on duty, Beatrice. I found this inside a museum on earth. Its soaked in magic and immortal magic."

Darkous handed Beatrice the fabric. She sniffed it and rubbed it with her hands. Sensing and feeling the magic flowing through the fabric. It was somewhat of a cinnamon scent to her.

"It is something powerful. Good that a human didn't come on

to this. There's enough magic in this fabric to cause a great catastrophe."

"By the way the magic surges through it and the power it possesses. It has to be Mazakala."

"Mazakala? I thought he was imprisoned in the deeper realm beneath us."

"His imprisonment expired some four hours back. I believe it was kept under wraps from causing a concern amongst us."

Beatrice put the fabric in her pocket and walked over to Darkous, hugging him and kissed him on the cheek.

"Very well, you must go and seek him out. I will remain here unless you contact me to aid you down in earth."

"Understand you well, Beatrice. I will call if needed."

Darkous teleports out of the Astral Dimension as if a gust of wind had picked him up and took him with it.

In Toronto, Ontario, Canada during the day, Supernatural Reporter Carol Hunters, a young attractive woman, who's countenance has brought about the wrong attention is investigating the series of murders. She has concluded the murders were done by a paranormal matter and the murders were caused by either ghosts or demons. Carol has been studying the paranormal for almost five years with some experience in the field. She has also come face to face with spirits and demons.

She is well known by sight from her long red-orange hair and her casual attire of a brown jacket and skirt with a white or black shirt at times. She also avoids wearing makeup, stating she doesn't like to wear animals on her face.

Carol searched the park, the downtown locations, the day cares, the schools, and the neighborhoods. She also spoke with some of the people that loss something in the murders and could barely get anything out of them.

"What do you know about the exact cause of your child's death?"

"We don't know. He was with us and we placed him to bed. We woke up the next morning and he was dead. Laying down in his bed peacefully."

"So, you do not know what if could've been?"

"We have no idea what could've done this. Maybe God decided it was the right time to take him."

"Only the matter will tell."

"They have no idea about the paranormal. Neither do they insist to know if it's a factor. These people are lost to themselves. Not understanding that something bigger is taking place all around us."

In the other parts of the world, particularly in Damascus, Darkous searches the ancient sites to find anything that will give him a signal to Mazakala's current whereabouts. The residents see Darkous searching the ancient grounds, they do not appear to be afraid of him, due to the awareness of the spiritual nature that surrounds the earth and the understanding of Darkous as a spiritual entity going about his business. Not finding anything with the wind blowing through his black hair and his dark violet trench coat and cloak.

"You are not this intelligent, Mazakala. No matter how much you perceive yourself to be knowledgeable."

"Darkous, I need to have a word with you."

Darkous heard the voice and understood its speech pattern. He shows a faint smile as he turned around and faced Michael the Archangel. Standing in front of him with glory beaming from his armor and wings. His skin glowing a dark bronze, his eyes appearing like a raging fire, and heavenly energy surging from his body.

"Michael, what is the word you have with me?"

"I know where Mazakala is located. But we must talk with each other someplace else. Not on earth."

"Where would you have us speak?"

Michael raised his head and gazed up above the clouds toward the clear sky. "Meet me in the Second Heaven and we can have our discussion there."

Michael flew up in the air with Darkous watched him on. He teleported from Damascus and into the Second Heaven.

II

SEARCHING FOR THE WANDERED

Michael and Darkous meet in the Second Heaven. The stars and worlds encamp around them. Darkous looked around seeing the sun in the distance and moon not too far from him. Darkous also glanced at the planets that were nearby and the meteors that moved on past them as if they were missiles.

"What is the word you have for me, Michael?"

"Mazakala is operating from various locations. He will make an appearance on the earth and will vanish. Afterwards, he'll show up in the dimensions and disappear, making a turn toward other places that exist in this universe."

"He's causing havoc and moving swiftly to avoid any kind of confrontation."

"What you'll have to do is outsmart him. He has been around for an eons time. But not as long as you have existed."

"Is he taking orders from someone or is he doing this all on his own?"

"He is taking orders. Small ones it appears from the ha-Satan."

"They're collaborating with each other? The two of them?"

"Satan gave him two allies. Their names are Kabra and Maba. They're demons who have committed a few of the smaller murders in the earth. They'll most likely have to be taken out before you can reach Mazakala. They appear to be his guards as well. When someone confronts him, Kabra and Maba are there for the attack and for the kill."

"I have some allies back on earth and in the Astral realm that can assist me on the two demons."

"As you are aware, Satan will need all the help he can get this day. He doesn't have much longer."

"You're right about that. I have been counting the hours that pass more so than before."

"The Elohim of Yisrael insists you find him before he causes something more troubling than murders in earth. Find Mazakala and defeat him for his imprisonment will be much longer than the last."

"I will do what I can to find him. I have a few places I believe he will make his way."

Michael nodded as he flew away like a flash of light. Darkous turned back toward the earth and evaporated like smoke, diving down toward earth and entering the atmosphere reaching the ground with the smoke coming together slowly, reforming Darkous in his physical form.

"I will need to speak with an ally of mine before I do this task."

At a meeting in Toronto, Carol stood by the wall, listening in on the men that are discussing various mythologies. The men insist the murders were caused by a mythological being. They vary in between mythologies, not knowing if the murderer is from the Greek and Roman, the Norse, the Hindu, the Japanese, the Chinese, the Celtic, the African, the Aztec, and other ideas. During their discussion, one of the men turned around, spotting Carol by the wall. She noticed his glare and tried to leave.

"Where are you going, lady?"

Carol stopped and turned to face them. The man waved his hand, insisting her to come to the table. She walked over to the table as the men turned and looked at her. She was somewhat fearful of the men as they appeared visually to be the mafia or some sort of crime mob due to the attire they wore. Traditional suits and coats with fedoras. Even smoking cigars.

"I take it you're some kind of reporter, huh?"

"I am."

"What are you reporting on?"

"The murders that have taken place over the few months."

"Oh. Really. So, what have you come up with on your investigations?"

"I believe the murderer was a paranormal entity. Like a ghost or a demon."

"I don't think so."

"What makes you say that?"

"There are many things which exist in this world, outside this earth, and throughout the universe and the dimensions that vary across it. We only know so little and it's the little that we should remain. But, there are those who seek more knowledge. Increasing our minds to fully understand the purpose of this world and universe."

"I did hear you gentlemen speak of the mythologies being the cause."

"Yes. We have a firm belief that the murderer is one of the various gods in the mythologies. We're not sure if its Thanatos also known as Mors in the Greek and Roman myths, Hel from the Norse, Kali from the Hindu, the Shinigami from the Japanese, Emperors of Youdu from the Chinese, Donn, the Dark One from the Celtics, the Ogbunabali from the Africans, Xipe-Totec from the Aztecs. Hell, it can even be some magical being like the Morrigan or it could be Azrael or some spirits traveling around."

"It could be the Evil One." One of the men said.

"Yeah. You're right. It could be."

"You guys know your mythology."

"Yes, we do. We know it so well for a singular purpose that most people seem to lack."

"Why would they lack it?"

"Because they don't study. They have too much time on their hands and what do they waste it on. The latest fashion trend or some low prices on items at a store. You've seen the Black Friday crowds and what they can do when it comes to buying materials. Imagine if they put that much effort into shaping their own minds and growing more in knowledge and wisdom. So much potential wasted on junk."

"Are you guys from around here?"

"We're natives of Canada of course. But we all were raised in different cities. We came together because we have a common mind and a common goal. To learn more and to grow in knowledge of the knowledge that is secret but can be grasp with much endurance and patience."

Carol looked at her watch, signaling for her to leave the building. She prepared to walk away, but the man called out to her again. She turned and approached him. He took a puff from his cigar before looking at her.

"Hopefully we'll see you again and maybe you can join in on our little conversations. Seems to me you have knowledge and soon it'll need to be spread out. Mainly among us."

"Another time then."

"Of course. Whenever you decide is the best moment for you. We won't hesitate. We'll wait patiently."

Carol left the room while the men continued with their conversation. Outside of the building, Carol walked down the sidewalk, looking through her phone to find information on the men she spoke with. Not finding anything connected to them, she placed the phone into her pocket and continued walking.

Out in the wilderness, Darkous stumbled upon an old large cabin. He walked up the stairs and approached the door. He knocked three times. He waited, and the door opened. Standing at the door was Darkous' apprentice. He bows to Darkous in servitude. A sign of respect.

"Master."

"Good to see you, Malach HaMavet."

"You here alludes to something that must be done."

"May I come in?"

"Sure."

Malach allowed Darkous to enter his cabin. Malach is a man after the African countenance. His physical appearance shows his potential in a battle. The interior of the cabin is a mixture of a home and a dojo. Darkous sat down in one of the chairs and Malach walked over, sitting in front of Darkous in the other chair.

"What is it this time, Master?"

"An immortal sorcerer known as Mazakala has been released from his imprisonment and is out causing havoc amongst the humans."

"You need me to assist you in taking him down?"

"I can handle Mazakala on my own. I need you to assist me on confronting his two soldiers that are in the way."

"Are they humans or something else?"

"Their demons. Kabra and Maba are their names and it appears they were given to him by the ha-Satan."

"So, he's involved in this as well."

"In a way. Just a small dose. I don't expect him to show us fully during all of this."

"Give me some time to prepare myself, Master and I will be ready to head off with you on this quest."

"Take your time to prepare, Malach. We have some time to spare."

Malach stood up and walked to his room to prepare his clothing and gear. Darkous stood by the window staring outside, looking at the sky and the trees and the grass. Out in the distance, he could see a strand of horses.

"They stand and eat. They stand and drink. They run when needed. They speed when applied."

Darkous turned and seen Malach prepared with his warrior clothing on and his sword at hand.

"I'm ready, Master."

"Let us head out toward our first place of business."

"Which is?"

"Finding Kabra and Maba."

"Won't we need a location to find them? I mean, they'll be somewhere I'm sure."

"The closer we get the Mazakala, the closer they'll be. Straightforward, they'll come to us."

Sitting in her home during the night, Carol sat at her desk reading books on the various mythologies. Most of them are the ones the men were spoke about. She read through the Greek and Roman myths, the Norse myths, the Hindu myths, the Japanese myths, the Chinese myths, the Celtic myths, the African myths, and the Aztec myths.

"There's so many possibilities that are around these murders. If only there was a single trail that I could trace it would make all of this easier than it could be."

She closed the books and placed them at the side of her desk while reading a paper that contained information on cosmic entities and astral dimensions. She rubbed her hand through her hair while reading and writing down notes.

During the night, Darkous and Malach walk through an abandoned town. Nothing in sight except fro debris and abandoned vehicles. Malach walked slowly while looking around his area. Darkous kept walking straight making no turns to look.

"What brings us here?"

"I can sense Mazakala's power here. Its strong."

"So, I can take the guess that he's here."

"He could possibly be or it is his residue that's left behind. Either way, he's closer than he was before."

Out in the distance, Malach saw a golden light flash. Malach pointed toward the site and Darkous looked toward it.

"I just saw a strange light appear from over there. Right by that building."

"Let us have a look."

They walked over toward the building. The building appeared to be a torn down church. They entered it and could find nothing in sight. Malach searched the place all around with his sword in hand. Darkous stood in the middle of the church and brought in the aura that was around. Malach walked back inside the church toward Darkous.

"Nothing. I couldn't find nothing."

Darkous stood still and silent.

"Master, what have you found? You seem to have found something."

"I've found…… I've found him."

"He's here?!"

"He is."

"Where is he, Master?! Let's finish this quest now."

"We will. But we have to face his company first."

"Where are they?"

"Right here."

From out of the air in a swivel of smoke, Kabra and Maba appeared before Darkous and Malach. Malach moved over avoiding a quickening slashing swipe from Maba. The two demons were disguting in appearance. Their eyes were like the sun and their smell was of sulfur. Their clothing appeared to be ripped and burned by a blazing heat. Even their rough skin appeared burnt with boils on their arms. Kabra lunged toward Darkous, grabbed by the throat. Choking him, Darkous stared him in the eyes. Showing the dominion between the two.

"So you're who he gave Mazakala. I expected more power."

"Don't underestimate our physical appearance, Shrouded One. We have to protect our general and protect him we shall."

"Very well. Protect him now. From me."

Darkous threw Kabra against the church's unsteady wall. Malach and Maba were having a swordfight amongst themselves with them going back and forth with attacks. Kabra got to his knees on the ground, seeing Darkous walking toward him slowly.

"You're taking this slowly. You're taking us for granted!"

"You don't possess the power to face someone like me. You've only been around for about a century. I have been around since the beginning."

Darkous kicked Kabra in the head and stomped his head into the wooden church floor. Kabra screaming with blood coming from his face. Darkous picked him up by his neck and tossed him against the wall once more.

"I expected Mazakala to give you a portion of his own power. Yet, he did not. Still selfish as he was before."

"Mazakala promised us much when he succeeds. He promised us power, lands, kingdoms, and servants."

"The typical materialistic nature of humanity has been washed upon demons. How oddly things have become."

Malach slammed Maba down on the ground with his sword and cut off Maba's left arm, dropping his sword in the process. Maba screamed in pain, holding his arm as his dark red blood gushed from the wound. The blood even smelled of sulfur and would burn the ground it touched.

"Didn't know demons could scream like that." said Malach. "Now to finish you off."

Maba pushed Malach away with some form of magic. Kabra began to use the magic against Darkous, attempting to consume him with a thick blanket of darkness. Darkous stood still as the darkness consumed him. Kabra smiled as Malach looked over seeing it happen.

"Master!"

"Now we know who is stronger than the other in the arts of darkness. I can consume you, Keeper of the Cosmos, I can consume anyone who gets in the way of Mazakala."

Maba ran over to Malach and punted him in the head, knocking him down. Maba picked up Malach's sword and started to walk toward him. Malach gazed his eyes on Maba approaching him, but also seeing Darkous covered in a thick darkness.

"Master?" Malach said with concern in his voice.

"With this newly received power, I will become the new

Keeper of the Cosmos."

"You think so?" Darkous said softly. "I do not."

The thick darkness immediate boasted away from Darkous and toward Kabra, who tried to keep it away from him with a magic force. Kabra pushed and pushed with all of his might. Maba looked on at Kabra pushing the darkness.

"You demons are all the same. You're all arrogant, proud, boastful, and selfish."

"Keep quiet!"

"You should understand something here, Kabra. Something that your general will soon come to understand as well."

"Get back! Get back!"

"Those who fear the darkness will dwell in darkness. Those who fear the light will succumb to the light. Either way, you'll fear."

Darkous raised his hand slowly and the darkness became like a beast and consumed Kabra, bringing him into total darkness to where he could neither see nor hear. Maba ran toward Darkous and Darkous turned to him and raised up his hand, pushing Maba against the wall and through a stake. Kabra's screams began to turn into silence. Darkous released Kabra from the darkness and it vanished into thin air, leaving Kabra on the ground motionless and silent. Malach retrieved his sword from Maba and walked over to Darkous.

"I didn't know what was going on, Master. I thought he had you for a second."

"I am the Keeper of the Cosmos. I control the darkness in this universe. I was created solely for that purpose."

They left the church, returning to Malach's cabin. While walking, Darkous stopped and gazed into the night sky taking witness to the stars above. Malach looked at him, sensing something taking place within the unseen realm.

"What is it, Master?"

"I am needed back at the Astral Dimension. I will speak to you again when it is time."

"Yes sir." Malach said with a bow.

Darkous disappeared into the night, appearing like dust flowing up above the air.

III

THE PLACE OF PURE DARKNESS

Darkous entered the Astral Dimension and sought his eyes on the person he seen standing in front of him. He levitated over toward them with anger in his eyes, which his while pupils are beginning to turn a dark red. He stopped and stared at who he was looking at. Lilu, one of the chief demons.

"Do you even want to test me in this dimension?"

"I do not wish to test you, Doctor of Mystics. That is not the purpose of why I'm here."

"Then why are you here, Lilu? I sensed trouble here and I come to find you here."

"I have come to bring word of Mazakala and what he has planned."

"Speak the word."

"Mazakala is making his move toward Sheol. He intends on using it for one of his plots."

"Why would he intend to use Sheol? How would he ever enter the realm."

"He has some help from the inside."

Darkous stared into the astral space, thinking to himself, silent. Lilu can only look at Darkous and wonder what is going on inside of his mind. Darkous returns to his conscious and glares at Lilu.

"I thank you for the information. Now, leave this dimension before I have to make you."

"I will leave at my own will, Darkous. But first I must tell you of an event that took place not too long ago on Earth."

"What kind of event have I missed that you have seen? It couldn't have been a major one."

"You remember Death? The young woman who's the sister of one of the Dark Gods?"

"I cannot forget such a twisted face. A face that humans would love and fear. A face that we dislike and destroy. She is all that they fear and love. Sad for the humans."

"She was apprehended in the city of Retropolis by some man wielding a divine sword. He brought her to their prison, and she is currently being held inside."

Darkous stood quiet.

"What do you want me to do about it?"

"What do you think I want you to do? Go and bring her back to where she belongs. With all of us."

"She made her choice to live amongst the humans and now she is paying for it. The man with the divine sword is no threat to us. I have known and seen the myths and legends of the sword he carries and the power it possesses. I have nothing to fear in him. But your kind surely should fear him."

"Here me out, I do not intend on freeing Death myself. But, she doesn't belong on the earth alongside the humans. She belongs with us here. On the Other Side."

"She made her decision. Besides, her goal is to free her brother from divine imprisonment. She already has the knowledge that he will be release when the imprisonment has been completed, and she can rejoice all she desires. Until then, Death is on her own. If I have the time, and I have the time to speak with her, I shall."

Darkous turned away from Lilu, he looked down and seen the pit toward Sheol. Preparing himself to jump into it, he glared at Lilu with his pupils glowing a dark gold.

"Now is your time to exit this dimension, Lilu. Return to your master."

"So, I can see. You'll be seeing me again sometime, Darkous."

Lilu warped into a wave of fire and flew out of the dimension. Darkous watched her leave before he took a leap down into the pit leading to Sheol. Diving down into the deep darkness to where no one can see or feel anything. Darkous' pupils turned to a dark blue, giving him the ability to see through Sheol's deep, thick darkness. He could also feel the darkness due to him being an Astral entity. Darkous landed on the grounds of Sheol with the dust rising The first thing he noticed are the cries and weepings of those that are trapped in the thick darkness. He looked around to see if anything was unusual than it should be.

"Why would you come to Sheol, Mazakala? What would be here for you that would enhance your already wasted power." Darkous said to himself.

Darkous walked through the darkness as he is the only one

there to be able to see through it clearly as if the sun was shining above him, showing him the steps. Darkous suddenly felt the pressure of the spirits that are trapped surrounding him. Their emotions were sad. Their tears could be heard dripping from the faces onto the ground like a faucet left turned. Their fear could be felt as well, consuming them that were around the other.

"I have a proposition for your spirits." said Darkous. "Have any of you heard or felt a magic unlike any other? A magic that's pressure was strong and heavy? An immortal magic?"

The spirits screamed out their answers and responses. Darkous listened to them very carefully. Trying to point out the ones that referred to magic and Mazakala. Darkous kept listening closely to the spirits.

"I need more than that. Do any of you know about Mazakala the Immortal?"

"I do." said a voice from behind. "I know about the Immortal Mazakala."

Darkous turned and seen the spirit of an elderly man approaching him. Darkous noticed the way he walked as if he could see where he was going.

"How have you learned to walk such a way in the thick darkness?"

"I have been here for a very long time, Cosmos Keeper. I have also seen the feats that you can do with this darkness and how terrifying it can be when you put it to its full potential."

"What do you know of Mazakala and of his supposed business down here?"

"Mazakala did come here not long ago, Darkous. He came

seeking information about cosmic power. A power that he intends to use against you and all the universe. He is angry of his imprisonment. Being set free will not heal that kind of bondage."

"I am aware. Mazakala put that bondage on himself and he knew the risks of his actions. Now he is repeating himself on a larger scale."

"Yes, he is. From what I could decipher, he was granted what he came for and is preparing for his full assault. Primarily against you and the others up there."

"That is his plan you say."

"That is his plan."

Darkous looked up toward the dim purple light that would lead out of Sheol and back into the Astral Dimension. He looked back at the elder spirit.

"Where is Mazakala headed now? If you know of it?"

"He's making his way toward Earth."

Darkous nodded to the man.

"Thank you for your pleasant conversation. Maybe you can be redeemed at the appointed time for your loyal help."

Darkous flew up in the air toward the dim purple light. Inching closer he flew through the light, returning to the Astral Dimension where he sees Beatrice standing by, waiting for him.

"Where have you been, Darkous?" She said with some curiosity.

"I've just returned from Sheol. Had a conversation with an elder spirit about Mazakala."

"Mazakala went into Sheol? For what? Information of some kind?"

"He went there to gain information on some sort of power. He apparently now has that power and is fully prepared to eliminate all of us from this universe from the lowest of us to the highest of all."

"What do you need me to do around here?"

"I need you to prepare yourself and anyone else around here to combat Mazakala if he makes his way here. The elder told me he was heading for Earth and I'm going there to confront him myself."

"Funny enough, I was about to tell you that you might need to go there for a small quest."

"What small quest is taking place?"

"Someone is trying to open up a portal in the city of Retropolis. If they open the portal, they will have entrance to the other worlds in the universe. This dimension as well as Sheol and possibly the Heavens."

"Be that as it may. I will handle this novice of a warlock in Retropolis and afterwards, I will find and confront Mazakala and end all of this. Period."

"Make sure you'll be careful if you come against him, Darkous. There's no telling what kind of power he now controls."

"You have a good point there, Beatrice. A good point."

Darkous vanished from the Astral Dimension, flowing through the air toward Earth.

Late in the night, Carol entered a nightclub, seeking possible information on spiritual events taking place inside the club. She witnessed men grouping on women and women grouping on men. Couples kissing in the corners of the club to almost having sex inside the club.

She could also see others sniffing cocaine and shooting themselves up with morphine to get high. She decided to stand in the back corner of the club, near the back-exit door. She watched the dancing take place with the loud music and the flashy light effects. Someone entered the club, everyone stopped dancing and stood still, getting Carol's attention, she also looked. The man who walked in was Malach with his sword in hand.

"I know you men work for Mazakala and I am here to kill you."

Six men stood out from the other clubbers who began to run out of the club. The men snarled at Malach and lunged toward him. Malach began to slice the men up with his sword, killing them one by one and some in pairs. Fighting the remaining two with kicks and elbow attacks. He impales one through the heart with his sword and chopped the head off the last one. The club is quiet when Malach sees Carol trying to exit the club through the back. From the bar corner, a man ran and grabbed Carol, trying to bite her. She screamed for help as Malach ran toward her and impaled the man through the back and cut off his head. He helped Carol to her feet.

"Are you hurt, Ms.?"

"I am ok. I don't know what's going on around here."

Malach noticed she carried notes and he gazed by, understanding her notes contained information of mythology. Uncertain of her place being inside some nightclub pass midnight hours for starters.

"Why are you here with notes on mythology?"

"I have… I have been on the study case of the recent murders in the past few months and I was aware that this club had contained some insight to the supernatural."

"Appears your insight was correct. These men work for the one who committed the murders."

"Wait. You know who the murderer is?"

"I need to take you to a safer location to avoid confronting him."

"Why would confronting him be a problem? By the way you fight, you can handle a simple murderer."

"The murderer is that simple. Besides, my Master is currently tracking him down."

"Your master?"

"I have the feeling you two will meet soon enough. I hope you're prepared for it."

"Doesn't look like I have any choice."

"From your notes, you don't have a choice in this matter."

The cold air blew through the city air of Retropolis and so did Darkous. Moving in the air faster than the vehicles below him on the streets. He looked around, sensing the located of the proposed portal opening. He turned his head to the left and looked, seeing a large prison. He senses the magic from inside the prison.

"There is the site of the magic."

Darkous landed on the ground and walked through the gates of Pegasus Prison. He walked slowly through the entrance of the gates, surrounded by their gardens and see some of the inmates sitting outside the place surrounded by Retropolis police officers. Darkous walked through the door and entered the prison. Inside he could feel the magic surging through the place from all corners. He concentrated and focused on the strongest place where the portal was trying to be opened.

"Third floor." Darkous' eyes glowed with light. "Seventh cell."

Darkous evaporated into specs of dust and went up through the floors to the third floor and flew toward the seventh cell. The dust formed back into Darkous' physical body as he looked inside the door, seeing the man playing around with magic trying to open up the portal.

"This has to stop now."

Darkous walked completely through the cell door as if he was a ghost. The prisoner turned, seeing Darkous inside the cell with him. Confused and uncertain, the prisoner pulled a knife from his cot and stood up against Darkous.

"You think I'm open! Not a chance pale boy."

"Enough playing around with magic, Cartavious Cage. I demand you cease your actions now."

"I am getting my ass out of this prison and there's nothing anyone can do about it."

"This is your final warning. Cease the magic."

"I will not. Who are you to tell me what to do? You're just a man. I can kill you right now and mark you as my next kill. Afterwards I will do wonders to your body to where not even the security will find your body. Your blood will be drained from this toilet here. I have my ways."

"And I have mine."

Darkous conjured up a dark hole that appeared behind Cage. He turned and tried to cut through it with his knife. Having no kind of effect period, Cage turned to Darkous and lunged at him with the knife. The knife hit Darkous in the chest, breaking in half. Cage looked at the knife and to Darkous who backhanded him against the wall, knocking him unconscious. Darkous walked over to Cage's magic spot, looking at what he was dealing with.

"A red gem, some crystal sand, and a grimoire. Where did you receive these items from inside of a prison?"

Darkous took the items with him and left the cell. While leaving, he could feel the presence of Death nearby. He continued walking until he appeared at her cell door. Looking inside, he could see her. Sitting in the corner laughing and giggling.

"You will never learn the rules, woman."

"Dark… Darkous……. Is that you?!"

"Get yourself in gear, Death."

"Gear. Ha. Gear."

Darkous teleported from the prison with the last thing he could hear was the laughter of Death.

IV

MATCHING CLUES

Malach and Carol returned to her home. When they enter, Malach noticed the table covered in books of many mythologies, some books are references for demonology, ancient religions, and modern religions. He walked over to the desk to have a closer look at the books. Carol locked the door and took off her jacket.

"You can make yourself at home."

"I will do that, ma'am."

Carol went to her refrigerator and pulled out a glass of water to drink. She looked at Malach going through her books.

"You want anything to drink?"

"I will take a small glass of water please."

Carol grabbed a glass and poured some water for him. She placed the pincher in the refrigerator and handed the water to Malach. He took a sip.

"Thank you."

Malach sat down at the couch with Carol sitting in the seat facing him. Carol looked around her home, checking the windows and the door again.

"Is this place safe enough?"

Malach looked around at the surroundings. Mostly the windows and the door. He nodded while taking another sip of water from his glass.

"It will do for the time being."

Malach looked at Carol for a moment. Finding the whole situation somewhat strange to her. Although it is a normal day for him.

"I know it may seem crazy to have a stranger in your home. Right now, we need to have a discussion. Primarily concerning you digging yourself into this field. Why did you choose this field to work in?"

"I have always been fascinated with the paranormal and the supernatural powers that shape our world. I've always known them to exist. I just, I just never had the opportunity of doing it in my earlier days."

"You don't appear to be as old as you're talking about."

"I'm only thirty-three and I wanted to start in this field right at twenty. Things don't always go the way you planned them out."

"They never do."

"So, why are you what you are? If that makes any kind of sense. I'm strictly speaking of you wielding a sword and battling foes of the supernatural. I've heard of such things, but I've never come to believe they were true."

"My name is Malach HaMavet. I am a warrior in the supernatural and I obey the Father above all."

"So, Malach, how did you come to entering the supernatural

field and becoming a swordsman?"

"When I was a young boy, I witnessed demons come from the shadow and kill most of my friends. My family thought I was nuts and called me a crack head, cook, cult leader, and a fantastic because of my testimony in confronting demons. They weren't exactly believers in the supernatural, but they went to church every Sunday to worship a supernatural deity. It wasn't until I decided to search the supernatural myself to understand what the demons were and where they came from."

"I take it you found out."

"I did. One day, I summoned the demons, the same demons who killed my friends. They came before me and we fought roughly. I was near-death, unable to combat them because of my ignorance in the supernatural. Suddenly, the room went dark and I couldn't see a thing, surprisingly neither could the demons see and I could hear their screams. Screams of fear and torment. I heard what sounded like a gust of wind had blown in from the windows and doors of the place and gathered them up and tossing them to the outside. Once the darkness had evaporated, I found myself staring face to face with the one who created the darkness. He told me I had courage and I had the Spirit to combat the demonic entities. So, he brought me in and trained me, taught me the supernatural realms and what is and what is not. Now, he is my Master."

"Who is your master?"

"My master in the art of the supernatural is known as Doctor Dark. He is the Keeper of the Cosmos and he watches over all of the darkness in the universe."

Carol showed a faint look on her face. Trying to understand how an entity of darkness could possibly help someone in need and even train them in the process to prepare their own selves.

"I always thought the darkness was evil and the light was good. Is there something I don't know?"

"There is a lot you do not know. I would hope that you could speak with Doctor Dark about it. He can answer all of your questions. Even the ones you haven't thought to ask."

"Where is he right now?"

"He's currently looking for Mazakala."

"So, he's the murderer?"

"He is and he's a very powerful warlock. He's basically immortal."

"An immortal warlock is responsible for the deaths that have taken place in the last few months? I would've never believed that to be the case."

"Mazakala has lived for eons and was temporarily imprisoned for his last actions in trying to open up the portals to the Heavens."

"Was he successful in trying to?"

"He could barely make a mark in the realms. Doctor Dark is on his trail and will eventually find him and put an end to his troubles."

"Will he need you to assist him?"

"If he contacts me, I will be needed. He hasn't spoken to me since we stopped Mazakala's demons in an abandoned town."

"He had demons under his control."

"They were given to him by Satan. Mazakala somewhat works

for Satan at this point. It explains how he's constantly getting away from confrontations in all parts of the universe."

Carol stared at Malach. Trying to put all this information in her head and to keep calm and relaxed.

"This is too much for you isn't it?"

"Right now, I could use a small break of the mind. You know. Let my brain rest for a bit."

Carol drank all her water and walked back to the refrigerator and grabbed a bottle of wine. She poured the wine in the glass and drank it.

"You know, if I may, I spoke with a group of men earlier and they had much knowledge of all this."

"What kind of men? Did they look like the ones in the nightclub?"

"No. They were well-dressed men. Not clubbing men. They would be the ones you would consider that would run the club from behind the scenes."

"You're saying they're businessmen type. Suits and hats. Smoking cigars probably."

"They were all of those. They spoke about various mythologies and who could the murderer be. They had spoken their opinions on who it could've been."

"I've heard of a group like that. I believe they call themselves the Mythologists. They work underground. Away from the rest of society. Keeping all the information they gain to themselves."

"They invited me back for another talk whenever I wished. They were very interested to know what I know."

"Best you let myself and my Master accompany you on your

next visit to see them."

"I shall do that."

Across the world, Darkous roamed through the cities and towns and counties and jungles and valleys and mountains searching for Mazakala. All Darkous had found are fragments of Mazakala's fabrics laying around at scattered locations. Darkous has collected the fabrics and remembers the locations of where they were placed.

"This is a set-up. He knows I'm looking for him and he's leaving behind nothing but breadcrumbs for me to pick up. Like I'm a dog to him."

Darkous traveled to Cairo, Moscow, Ethiopia, Jerusalem, Damascus, the Sahara Desert, Sydney, Australia, Scandinavia, Ukraine, Germany, Turkey, Palestine, India, China, North Korea, South Korea, the Amazon Rainforest, Tokyo, Mecca, the remains of Ur, Mount Ararat, London, Paris, New York, Chicago, Los Angeles, Miami, Little Rock, New Orleans, Houston, Dallas, Phoenix, Newark, Enigma City, Retropolis, Seattle, Vancouver, the Northern Mountains. All of those places is where Darkous had discovered the fabrics of Mazakala.

"He intends on invading these places to attack them. To turn them into nothing but rubble where he will be the only one to rise them up from their ashes."

Darkous collected all of the fabrics he could find and was not unaware of what he needed to do next. Uncertain of his next move, Darkous decides to return to the Astral Dimension to uncover more clues as to where Mazakala is heading next on Earth. Darkous vanished out of thin air and went to the Astral Dimension.

Upon arriving there, he discovered the place was attacked. He looked around and found Beatrice laying on the ground.

"Beatrice!"

Darkous levitated with speed over to her and held her up. Rubbing her face with his glowing hand.

"I can sense you're still alive. Wake up for me now, Beatrice. Wake up now."

Beatrice awoke and looked around, gaining back her conscious. Immediately she noticed Darkous in front of her, holding her.

"Darkous. What are you doing here? I thought you were supposed to be on Earth."

"What happened here is the real question. What happened here, Beatrice. What took place here for me to find the place in ruin and you lying on the floor unconscious?"

"I... I... I don't remember. All I can recall is me searching for the whereabouts of Mazakala and this bright light appear and that was it. Next thing I saw was you holding me."

"Someone must have invaded the realm. We need to be on guard."

"They could still be in here, Darkous. Somewhere around here."

"That is what I'm telling you. I can sense some form of energy in here and it isn't native to this place. It's something else entirely and I will purge it out of this place."

The bright light returned and knocked Darkous and Beatrice to the floor. The light inched closer toward them and dimmed down. Darkous looked toward it to see who was in control and he knew who was in control of the light. Darkous showed a small grin on his face as his pupils turned a dark red.

"It's about time we meet again."

"Yes, it is time."

The light dimmed, and it was Mazakala who invaded the dimension. He stared down Darkous. Mazakala's hairy structure showed off its golden color and his golden horns. He levitated off the ground holding two daggers in his hands. Darkous stood up and stared at Mazakala. The anger surging through him.

"All the mess you have caused on Earth, you bring here."

"This is your place isn't it, Keeper of the Cosmos. I fully intended on paying you a visit when I was released from my imprisonment."

"You understand that one of us will die on this day."

"I do, Darkous. I do and we both know who will survive this bout and it certainly won't be you. I will kill you by snapping your neck in two. I will absorb your darkness and become the new Keeper of the Cosmos and I will rain down darkness upon the earth and after that the universe and lastly, the Heavens. When that is done, I will be the new God. The new Elohim."

"You're finished now, Mazakala. There's no turning back for you now. You are living in your last moments. From this moment forward, when I get my hands on you, you will wish that you were still imprisoned. For the beating that I will give you will be unlike any attack you have felt in the eons of your days. Are you ready for it, Immortal One?"

"I am prepared for what may come of this battle and I am ready."

"As am I."

V

DIMENSIONAL WARFARE

Darkous and Mazakala clashed one another with their power. The power of darkness battling it out with the power of magic. Mazakala used his daggers to create a wave of magic beams that attacked Darkous. Darkous turned toward him and raised his arms, creating a dark ball and threw it toward Mazakala, knocking him back. Mazakala looked and seen Darkous flying toward him with a punch. Darkous punched Mazakala and backhanded him against the illusionary wall of the Dimension.

"You are strong as you've always been, Darkous."

"Enough words."

Darkous kicked Mazakala in the head and rammed his fist down on Mazakala's skull, imprinting a hole in the floor. Mazakala kicked Darkous back and grabbed him by his coat and threw him against the wall and slammed him on the floor. As Darkous gets to his feet, Mazakala flies up in the air, trying to escape and Darkous chased him. They fly and battle through the wormhole. Punching and kicking one another.

"Seems we're heading to Earth, Darkous! Ready to see what I have prepared down there?!"

"You have nothing down there!"

"Oh! We shall see if your words are as true as you believe them to be!"

Meanwhile on Earth, Carol and Malach are walking down a sidewalk in Toronto when suddenly a pair of black-clad soldiers appear from a portal in the middle of the street. The civilians run with fear as the soldiers began to tare apart cars with their strength.

Blocking traffic, the soldiers began destroying the cars and killing the people inside of them. Malach put his arm in front of Carol. The soldiers' eyes glowing red as they slowly began to walk toward Malach and Carol on the sidewalk.

"What are they?!"

"Don't run Carol! I may need your assistance on this one."

"How would you need my assistance?! I don't have a sword in my possession."

Malach reached down over to his side and pulled up his sheathe and handed it to Carol. She looked at it confusingly as the soldiers spotted them and started walking toward them.

"Give me your sheath?! This won't do anything."

"Hold it outward and turn it to the right."

"Why?"

"Just do it and see what will happen."

Carol held out the sheathe in front of her and turned it to its right. The sheathe began to shake and from it formed a sword of its own. Now, Carol had possession of a sword. She smiled while looking at the sword she was holding.

"That was? That was very unusual."

"Now, I need you to help me stop them before they kill more people. Can you do that?"

"I can now."

Malach and Carol run toward the soldiers who do the same. They collide with Malach impaling and cutting the heads off many soldiers. Carol blocked the attacks from the soldiers and stabbed as many as she could in the chest toward their hearts. They kept fighting as more soldiers began to show up through portals opening in the street.

"Just keep fighting, Carol! We can handle these soldiers!"

"Why can't you just call your master down here to aid us?!"

"He's busy with greater matters. We have to deal with the problems here!"

"Sure."

They continue fighting the soldiers. Swiping, impaling, and cutting off the heads of the soldiers they combat against. From the air view, it looked like there were over a dozen or so soldiers standing in front of Malach and Carol.

Above them, Darkous and Mazakala continue to brawl with punches and kicks. Darkous grabbed Mazakala by the throat and started pummeling him in his face. Mazakala shot some form of magic in Darkous' face. Blinding him for a small time. Mazakala laughed out loud.

"You can't see what I'm about to do next!"

Mazakala kicked Darkous, ramming him into the grounds of the desert. Darkous rubbed his eyes and could barely make out anything with his sight. What he could make out were a set of pyramids in the distance. He knew where they were.

"We're on Earth. We're in Egypt."

"Yes, we are, Darkous. We're in Egypt. One of the places where I will destroy all that sits here only to rebuild it in the image of Mazakala."

"I will not allow this to happen."

"What can you do, Darkous. You can't barely see what's going on. What can you really do."

Mazakala punched Darkous and grabbed him by his long black curly hair and slammed in in the dirt. Mazakala started to stomp Darkous deeper into the ground. Stomp after stomp after stomp, Darkous goes deeper into the ground as if Mazakala is stomping him into his own grave.

"Have you ever been buried alive, Darkous. I would think you have but it wouldn't affect you. The darkness wouldn't bring fear to you. You would use it for strength and would eventually burst from the grave, stronger once more. Not this time, Darkous. This time, you will die, and I will be the one to have killed you."

"I will not easily go down to you, Mazakala. No matter how much stronger you've become because of your allegiance with the ha-Satan."

"Satan. Oh! He's helped me very well. Gave me some power I could never have possessed if it wasn't for me opening up the door to my anger and rage. He helped me and I'm helping him."

"Figured you would say something like that. Still the weak immortal that you are."

Mazakala kicked Darkous in the face and started to stomp him in the face into the ground.

"This is where you truly belong, Keeper of the Cosmos. Underneath my heel."

Darkous pushed the foot of Mazakala off of his face and punched him. Slowly getting to his feet, Mazakala rammed him with a spear and summoned cobras with his magic. Mazakala directed the cobras to Darkous.

"Feast upon him, my creations! Feast upon the Darkness of the Darkness."

Darkous fights off the large cobras as the circle around him. He grabbed one by the head and ripped it apart. The other cobra slithered around Darkous and was able to snatch him and constricted him.

"You're weakening, Darkous. Looks like your time is about to be up. No more Darkous."

Malach and Carol continue to take down the remaining soldiers. Slicing them apart and impaling them as they fall to the pavement. Malach chopped the heads off of the ones that laid on the road while Carol impaled them in the heart. Malach looked ahead seeing the last remaining soldiers running toward him.

"There's three left, Carol. Let's finish this."

"Sure thing, Malach."

They ran toward the three soldiers and instantly Carol impaled the three together on the sword. She took a few steps back from them. Malach looked and saw what she had done. An idea had come to his mind.

"I can finish this."

Malach walked over and chopped the heads off the soldiers. Their bodies fall to the ground and Carol retrieves her sword. She looked around and all she could see was the bodies of the soldiers. Dead. Civilians started to show up from around corners and peeking from buildings and doorways.

"It's done. We did it."

"Yes, we did."

Carol handed the sword back to Malach.

"Here."

"Thank you. You're not bad with a sword."

"I had to learn very quickly. Never used a sword before for anything."

"Always a first for everything they say."

As they talk with one another, behind them is the museum and through the windows, stand the group of men that Carol spoke to. They stand, looking outside toward her and Malach. Smoking cigars. The leader shook his head.

"The woman knows something we don't. We'll have to get her back in here somehow and as soon as possible."

Back in Egypt, Mazakala is overpowering Darkous as the cobra is sucking the breath from Darkous' body. Mazakala is conjuring up more magic and throwing it toward the cobra, giving it strength and squeeze Darkous even more.

"Not much longer, Darkous and you'll be out of breath."

"I… still have….the fight… within me."

"No, you don't! Your time has come, and you won't accept it. The time is here and there's nothing that you can do about it."

"Maybe I can."

Mazakala heard the voice and was blown back by a wall of energy. The cobra was hit and flew across the desert. Darkous fell to the ground, regaining his breath. He raised his head and seen Beatrice standing in front of him, holding up a green gem.

"Good to see you here." Darkous said.

"I figured you'll need some assistance with this one. Besides, I want some payback of my own."

Mazakala rubbed the sand off his face and seen Beatrice walking toward him. He smiled and stood up to his feet. He pointed at Beatrice with anger behind it.

"If you think me laying you out on the dimensional floor wasn't enough. Prepare to witness what I can do with the power I know possess."

"Show me what you can do, Mazakala." Beatrice said with a smile. "Prove it to me, you bastard."

Mazakala forms a cloud of magic above them. The cloud is intense that lighting is forming from within it. Beatrice stared at the cloud and so does Darkous.

"He's stronger than before, Beatrice. It will take the both of us to combine our power to match his. That appears to be the only way that we'll have to defeating him."

"When we do defeat him, are we imprisoning him again or can we just kill the guy?"

"You know that's not up to me."

Beatrice shrugged.

"Meh. You're right."

She raised the gem, holding it high above her and Darkous. She smiled toward Mazakala. He could see the smile and it was sending him into a rage, thinking they were taking his power as a joke.

"This isn't a game, woman!"

Mazakala throws the ball of magic toward them. The lightning sparking and surging within it as it moved through the air.

"Feel the power of the Immortal One!"

Darkous raised his hands up toward the ball. He looked to see what Beatrice was doing and she was only standing still with the gem still above their heads. Darkous was confused about what she was doing.

"What are you plotting, Beatrice?"

"Trust me on this one, Darkous. Just wait for what you're about to witness here this day."

The magic ball inched closer toward them with Darkous slowly creating a shielding to protect them. Beatrice noticed the shielding and turned to him.

"If you're going to shield us, do it and leave the gem in the open."

"Why would I do that?"

"Because this gem isn't no ordinary gem, Darkous. Once the ball hits, you will find out what it is made of."

Darkous shielded them except for the gem as the ball slammed against them. The magic ramming against Darkous' shielding.

They could hear the laughter of Mazakala coming from behind the shielding. Darkous, still weakened, holds up his strength against the ball. Beatrice holds her own against the ball in the shield.

"You two are finished. You won't be able to stop that much power. No matter what your positions are in the universe."

The ball touching the gem. The gem glows and absorbed in the magic ball completely within seconds. The area is quiet as Darkous released the shielding and looked toward the gem. Beatrice held the gem closely. Mazakala is confused as to what happened to his ball of magic and lightning. The gem continued its glow.

"Where did you get retrieve that object?"

"A friend gave it to me, and I know what it's for."

"What has just happened?!" Mazakala yelled. "Where is my orb of magic?!"

Beatrice looked up toward Mazakala and held up the gem. She smiled.

"Right here."

The gem shook and from the gem came forth the orb of magic, heading straight for Mazakala. Fearful for what has happened, he tried to hold it back with his strength. Yelling and pushing.

"This is not happening to me!"

The orb of magic consumed Mazakala as he yelled in pain. Feeling the lightning striking him. The orb evaporated and Mazakala crashed to the ground. Darkous and Beatrice walked toward him as he shook the disturbance of the lightning from his body. He glared toward them with anger.

"I feel somewhat different. But that will not stop me from killing the two of your right where you stand."

"Go ahead. Kill us, Mazakala. With all of your powerful might."

Mazakala held his hand out and began to recite a spell. The spell became intense that his hand started to glow. With the final words of the spell, a bright light came from his hand and immediately dimmed out like a light bulb. Shocked, Mazakala looked at his hand and tried again. Still no effect.

"What has happened to me?"

"Your power has been zapped away from you. The power you once had is stored inside this gem. I know. It hurts."

"This cannot be possible."

Beatrice turned to Darkous. He looked at her and smiled.

"You can finish him off now."

"As I may."

Darkous raised his hands above him and the sky immediately turned into darkness. Mazakala looked round and could only see Darkous and Beatrice. He tried wiping away the darkness that surrounded them.

"What is going on? What are you doing, Darkous?"

"This is your final end, Mazakala."

"It is not."

"Yes, it is, dumbass." Beatrice uttered. "Deal with it."

"You whore of an Astral!"

From the sky came down a blanket of thick darkness, falling directly over Mazakala. He stared, swiping it away from him. But the blanket is so thick it cannot be moved. Its touch is rough, yet, warm and cold. A mixture of the strangeness.

"I will not allow this to happen to me! I am Mazakala! I am the Immortal One!"

"You are Mazakala. Yes. But I am Darkous, the Keeper of the Cosmos."

The blanket consumed Mazakala as he tried to fight back against the darkness.

"I will give you comfort in the blanket of darkness. A comfort that you will not enjoy. A comfort that will eat you alive for all of eternity. This is my immortal gift to you."

"NO!"

"Now, accept your comfort."

Mazakala instantly goes unconscious in the blanket of darkness. Beatrice hugged Darkous.

"Now what do we do about him?"

"We'll take him to the Council. See what they will do with him."

"I'm with that."

Darkous and Beatrice disappear along with the darkness blanket and Mazakala in tow from Egypt.

VI

THE ATMOSPHERE ABOVE US

A sentencing was held for Mazakala as he was sentenced to the pit of Sheol until the appointed time for his releasing, which will be his final time. While leaving the sentencing, Darkous received a message from an anonymous messenger. He opened the letter and read it. The letter only said,

"Darkous, you are hereby to appoint to The First Heaven for discussion of Mazakala's actions on Earth."

"I have to pay him a visit. Should be interesting."

Darkous vanished and entered The First Heaven. Looking down at ground, seeing people going to and fro of their business. He continued to walk toward the throne room. The guards moved as he entered. They closed the door afterwards and Darkous stood there, staring at the chair.

"You wanted me."

"I did."

The chair turned and Darkous is staring at the ha-Satan. Tall and strongly built. He signaled Darkous to approach him. Darkous slowly moved toward him, being cautions of his surroundings.

"Still see you're here."

"Where else can I go to get a good view of humanity. The Father's most precious creation."

"That still bothers you doesn't it."

"I am the favorite creation. I am the greatest of all creations and yet, I was cast out and banished here on Earth. Yet, your kind, you Astrals, continued to go around doing your own business at your own risks."

"We do what we are created to do. We were all created for a purpose and you ruined yours."

"I did not call you here to start an argument about our places in the universe. I called you here because of what you've done to Mazakala."

"It is a shame that you brought him into your inner circle and look where that has placed him."

"No. No. No. Mazakala's own actions placed himself into the pit of Sheol. There are others in this universe, Darkous that are stronger and more cunning than Mazakala. Hell, they're even smarter than he is."

"I'm surprised you didn't call one of them up to do this line of work for you. Going around killing innocents."

"You know none of them were innocents. Do any of them

keep the truth and the Law in their hearts. You already know the answer to this."

"Get to the point of why you called me here."

Ha-Satan nodded with a grin.

"Sure. I called you here to thank you."

"Thank me for what?"

"For showing me that Mazakala wasn't the right one for the jobs ahead. You've shown me there are more out there willing to do the jobs and succeed in doing them. I love your way of working."

"Whatever you intend on plotting next, I will be there to stop it."

"I'm counting on it, Darkous. You may leave now."

The doors opened and Darkous leaves the throne room and flies out of The First Heaven, going down toward the Earth.

After about a week, Darkous walked through Retropolis during one of their rainy nights. The thunder cracks above him in the night sky with lightning clashing against one another across the sky of the city. Darkous could hear the sirens of the police cars zooming down the streets. He could also hear them on their communication speakers.

"We have a suspect in tow." said an officer.

"Why don't we just let The Swordman deal with them?"

"Because he's a myth. Been reading folklore have you."

"Always they argue over what they don't understand. Humanity." Darkous said to himself. "They never cease to amaze me.”

Darkous entered one of the alleyways and stumbled upon Death. Who's standing in front of him wearing her black trench coat. her face as pale as it could ever be with her black-colored lips and her green eyes. Confusion ran through the head of Darkous. He wondered to himself but decided to ask her of the situation in order to comprehend the meditation of what is taking place.

"How did you get out of the prison?"

"I have friends all over the place, Darkous. You know how I operate things. How did you know I was in the prison?"

"Lilu told me about it. You do understand that I will have to take you back there, right?"

"I'm not going back to Pegasus, Darkous. I am not going back. I have business to do at this moment."

"Does this business contain information about your Dark God of a brother?"

"It does a little bit. But, you see, Darkous, I want revenge against the man who put me in that prison to begin with. I also am aiding others that insist on taking down these heroes that have risen over the past three years. We are prepared to do anything to stop them."

"Very well. Just know that I will not interfere with your little task of causing chaos. But if it does become a larger threat than will threatened the universe, I will come for you and I will stop you."

Death laughed at Darkous. She walked over toward him and patted him on his shoulder.

"You are funny."

Darkous stared at Death with uncertainly in his eyes. Death continued to smile at him and giggle a bit.

"I'll be seeing you around, Death. You can guarantee that."

"I will surely do so."

Darkous evaporated along with the rain and vanished. Death looked around and walked away down the alley, laughing to herself.

"The time is right. The time is right. Hope your prepared for the fight is pared."

ABOUT THE AUTHOR

Ty'Ron W. C. Robinson II is the author of several works of fiction. Including the *Dark Titan Universe Saga* series (*Dark Titan Knights, The Resistance Protocol, Tales of the Scattered, Tales of the Numinous, Day of Octagon*) and *The Haunted City Saga* series. Also of other books (*Lost in Shadows, Hod, The Book of The Elect, Symbolum Venatores, etc.*) and One-Shot short stories More information pertaining to the author and stories can be found at darktitanentertainment.com.

www.ingramcontent.com/pod-product-compliance
Lightning Source LLC
Chambersburg PA
CBHW021154110726
47900CB00002B/567